The Merang Mysteries

The books can also be read as standalone

The Murder Before Merangs

The Merang Mysteries

Carole Marples

Published by Carole Marples, 2022.

THE MURDER BEFORE MERANGS

First edition. January 1, 2022.

ISBN: 979-8223906988

Written by Carole Marples.

To all at Scribophile

Dead Body at Donny's

On Saturday morning, Tracy found me rinsing a knife at the sink with a bloodied corpse near my feet. Near my pink plastic roller skates, to be more exact.

'Oh God, Helen.' Tracy's voice wobbled. 'What have you done now?'

As I spun around to face her, my curls caught in my mouth. 'What do you mean? I'm just washing this knife I found in—'

'You should have left it ... there ... in the body.'

Body? What's she talking about?

A fly landed on Tracy's pink, shiny cheek. 'Put the knife back in the sink and step away. There's a good girl.'

I'm thirty, for God's sake.

Tracy, my manager at Donny's Doughnuts and Diner, had always talked to me as if I were twelve. I swallowed my irritation and did as she said. Strange as it sounds, that was when I first registered the body lying at the side of the sink. My knees shook as I realised it must have been dried blood on the knife and not jam. I screamed.

Tracy jumped and backed away. With a trembling plump hand, she pulled her phone from her bag and called the emergency services.

The police soon arrived in a whirl of blue lights and with a no-nonsense attitude. Before you could say jam doughnut, they'd slapped the cuffs on my shaking wrists. Outside, I kept my head down – more out of embarrassment at my attire than anything else. Only three months before, I'd strutted London's financial corridors of power; the heels and designer outfits reflecting my high-flying status. Back up North, I whisked between greasy tables wearing a ra-ra skirt and roller skates. How the mighty had fallen. Several times on my arse, in fact. That's why I'd gone in early to practise.

I'd probably only got the job because of my stupid idea about skates. Donny Doughnut himself had gatecrashed the interview, just as his wife was about to eject me.

My interview with Pauline Donoghue had started badly. Raising her heavy-lidded eyes from my application form, she'd said, 'You use the title, "Ms"?'

So what? 'Yes.'

She sniffed and gave a toss of her lank hair as if I were claiming to be the great Dowager Duchess of Leeds. Perhaps she'd like me to call her Dame Doughnut? I fought to suppress a laugh. I needed this job.

Returning to my application, she said, 'I see you've had relevant experience.'

'I'm barista-trained,' I half lied. 'I'm a coffee fanatic.' True, but what a lame thing to say.

My experience had been mainly on the customer side of the counter in Woofs, my favourite cafe back on the Isle of Dogs. On weekdays, I had an early morning coffee before my short walk to the office, another on my way home, and then brunch there every Saturday with Zack. That was when Becky, the owner, allowed me to operate the coffee machine.

For someone I barely knew, Becky had been incredibly kind. Witnessing my disintegration after Zack walked out, she put up with me haunting her cafe, gave me simple jobs as a diversion, and then agreed to aid and abet my white lie.

'Woofs.' Pauline curled her thin, disapproving lips around the name. 'I see you worked there for two years. Why did you leave?'

I took a deep breath. 'Oh, you know, living in London, the pace of it all. I missed the North. I wanted to come back home.'

She pushed the steel-rimmed glasses up her long nose. 'But, I see from your application, Leeds isn't home to you.' Her tone suggested she might need to check my passport.

'Well, Buttersley's only twenty or so miles away.' I emphasised my Yorkshire accent. 'But, as you probably know, it's a bit of a backwater. I'm a city girl now.'

'So, *Ms* Merang, why do you want to work at Donny's Doughnuts and Diner?'

It was the question I'd prepared for the most. I'd planned to prattle on about how I'd be thrilled to join an exciting new concept, to be part of a pioneering team in the world of deep-fried confection. But a glance at the stern face opposite put me off my stride.

'I ...' My mouth stayed open. A single tear ran down my face.

Pauline's eyes flickered, and she fidgeted with her pen. 'Can I get you a glass of water?' If she'd not softened her tone, I might have held it together, but that bare hint of kindness opened my emotional dam.

The tears flowed, and my nose ran. Searching frantically through my bag for a tissue, I tipped the contents onto the desk. My lucky marble rolled off the edge, a half-eaten oat bar crumbled, and dark hairs fell from my brush.

'Ms Merang. I really—'

'Sorry, sorry. You must think I'm mad, but my husband left me. He walked out one day, and I've not heard from him since. I ... I need ...'

The woman I'd thought cold and austere surprised me. She came to my side of the desk, laid a hand on my shoulder and placed a tissue in my hand. 'We've all got our crosses to bear, my dear. I'll leave you for a moment to compose yourself and get you a cup of tea.'

'Thanks. That's very kind of you.' As she closed the door, my face burned. Four months after Zack had gone, I was still a mess and couldn't even get a job in a cafe. At the bank, I'd jumped before being pushed. The tricky and complicated issues I'd once handled with ease had suddenly become hardcore sudoku. And I'd made the mistake of trying to carry on as if nothing had changed. What a fool.

By the time Pauline returned, I'd managed to regain my composure. Although she smiled and patted my shoulder, we both knew she wanted me off the premises ASAP. Who in their right mind would employ such a wreck?

That was when Donny Doughnut had popped his head around the door. 'You see, Helen,' he'd said, rapidly blinking his currant-coloured eyes, 'it'll be like a sixties' American diner here in Leeds city centre: red leatherette booths, a black and white tiled floor, Elvis on the jukebox. I'm getting the memorabilia shipped over as we speak.'

'Oh, wow,' I said, cranking up my enthusiasm. 'Will the waitresses be zipping around on roller skates?'

His moustache did a quick jig. 'Certainly. That's one of my better ideas.'

Pauline coughed. 'I don't know about that, Donald. Think of the insurance. All those potential accidents and claims.'

'Oh, *we* don't worry about all that, do we, Helen?' He placed his small, plump hand on my shoulder. 'You're just the sort of smart young lady we're looking for. When can you start?'

My turn to blink. I swivelled back to face Pauline and caught the sneer of disdain. I couldn't tell if it was for me or her husband.

If only he hadn't intervened, I wouldn't be facing a murder charge.

A Duck to Skates

Staring through the grimy window of the police car as we raced through the streets, I considered my predicament. Strange as it might seem, being arrested for murder was not my major concern. Not then, anyway. No, what I fretted about most was my upcoming performance on skates. I imagined the police station to have an enormous, highly polished floor, designed to make roller skating felons think twice about their crimes. The arresting officer would give me a big push at the door, and I'd pinball from wall to wall before collapsing in front of an ancient judge wearing the black cap of death.

I'd been the worst skater at our first training session just one week before. In a stuffy room over the shop, I met my colleagues on the team.

'Hi, I'm Gloria.' A woman with a mass of blonde curly hair and freckles grinned and held out her hand. 'They've told us to wait over here.' She flicked her lively blue eyes to the corner where Donny, Pauline, and a young, stocky woman seemed to be arguing.

I shook her hand. 'I'm Helen. I've met Donny and Pauline. Is that their daughter? She looks like Donny.'

'Yeah, Tracy. She's Donny's daughter from his first marriage. Pauline is wife number three.' Gloria stepped aside to reveal a young girl with fearful eyes who'd been hiding behind her. 'This is Jade. She's on our team. A bit nervous though, aren't you, love?'

Jade bowed her mousey-coloured head.

I smiled. 'Oh, so am I. Try not to worry. It's new to us all.'

Gloria nudged her. 'Hey, it'll be a laugh. Wait till my kids find out I've been let loose on roller skates; they'll be *so* embarrassed. It's bad enough their mum's working in a diner. Teenagers, you know.' She gazed at the ceiling and shook her head.

I gasped. 'Gloria, you don't look old enough to have teenagers.'

She linked her arm in mine. 'Helen, you're my best friend already.'

I didn't have a chance to reply, as our employers were heading towards us. Pauline carried a large box, Donny held his arms open wide, and his daughter clutched a clipboard.

Donny clapped his hands. 'Ladies, ladies, how delighted I am to welcome you into our big, happy family. We are the Donoghues, loud and proud.' His moustache quivered, and his piggy eyes beamed as if he'd won a million pounds.

Gloria whispered, 'Pauline looks like she wants to stab him.'

Pauline had done her dark hair up in a loose bun. I don't know about Pauline wanting to stab her husband, but from the rigid set of her mouth, she didn't look happy. I surmised the box contained our roller skates, and she'd had one last go at trying to deter him.

Donny pushed his daughter forward. 'This is Tracy, my shop manager. Consider her your wise, big sister. That's our management style at Donny's Doughnuts and Diner.' He rolled out the name as if it were the most famous brand in the world.

Gloria spluttered like she'd eaten a dodgy prawn. 'Sorry, everyone.' She gave an exaggerated cough and thumped her chest. 'I don't know what happened there.'

Pauline settled the box on the floor, and Donny dived in to pull out glittery roller skates and some frilly nylon tat.

'Look, ladies.' Donny held up a minuscule pink dress with a ra-ra skirt attached. 'You're going to look the bee's knees.'

I'd have loved it if I were ten.

'I'm going downstairs to check on the builders,' said Pauline.

'Tell 'em to get their skates on, my love.' Donny chuckled. 'Ladies, you'll have to get used to my sense of humour.' He turned back to Pauline. 'They're cutting it fine for our grand opening.'

As Pauline left the room, Tracy moved closer to Donny. Her leopard-print heels brought her level with him. She was just as rotund as her dad, but with plenty of cleavage.

Donny threw an arm around her shoulder. 'Talented Tracy, I call this one. She's personally designed your gorgeous uniforms.'

Gloria made that choking sound again. I wanted to join in.

'Ever since being an itsy-bitsy little thing,' Donny continued, 'she's had a passion for pink.'

Tracy parted her magenta lips to expose small, uneven teeth. 'I've gone for a pastel shade to blend with the doughnut toppings. It couldn't be just any old pink.' She addressed the last bit to me, with a glare, as if I were about to challenge her colour wheel expertise.

'My Tracy thinks of everything. She's got such an eye for detail.'

Tracy fluttered her false lashes before father and daughter beamed at each other. Never having known a dad, a pang of envy ran through me at their mutual adoration.

'Okay, ladies,' Tracy said in a brisk tone. 'I want you to try on your uniforms in the stockroom.' She pointed to a door at the back. 'Don't take forever. And then we'll start your skating practice. I've set out the tables with crockery to make it as realistic as possible.'

In the stockroom, surrounded by giant tubs of jam and icing, we wriggled into our flimsy, unforgiving uniforms.

'I think they've given me the wrong size,' said Gloria. 'This wouldn't fit a doll.'

'I've just about got into mine,' said Jade in a quiet voice.

Gloria raised a flushed face. 'Wow, Jade, get you. This trash could only look good on someone your age. You look—'

'Pretty hot,' I said.

The girl blushed. 'It's so tight, I can hardly breathe.'

'Well, love, you're gonna bust your seams laughing at me,' said Gloria. Red-faced and groaning, she took a deep breath. 'That's if I ever get the damn thing on.'

Jade moved towards her. 'Let me help.'

She stretched the opening of the tubular top over Gloria's heavy curls until it hung loosely around her neck, with the frilly skirt resting on her shoulders.

Copying Jade's technique, I managed to drag the top over my own mass of curls, but then stared in dismay at the clump of dark hair that had caught in the skirt.

'Wow, Helen. You look pretty hot yourself.' Jade stepped back. 'That's it. Gloria, you're in.'

'Thanks, love. You're a star. I'm hoping it'll stretch for next time. This material's so bloody itchy, and I'm gonna stink after an hour.'

'The colour suits you,' I said, not wanting to draw attention to her lumps, bumps, and bulges.

Gloria tugged down the skirt. 'I'd like to see Talented Tracy in one of these.' She placed her freckled arms on our shoulders and drew the three of us together. 'Don't know about the other staff, but we are the A-team. The best.'

In that stuffy stock room with two strangers, stuffed into over-tight, tasteless uniforms, a chink of happiness poked through the misery of the last few months.

Jade pulled away first. 'Tracy told us not to be long.'

By the time we emerged, Donny had disappeared. Tracy didn't comment on the uniforms. Her eyes narrowed at Gloria before reverting to her clipboard. She failed to hide the faint smirk on her slug-shaped lips, and I hoped Gloria hadn't noticed.

Clapping her hands, Tracy trotted to the centre of the room. 'I've laid out your skates. As soon as you can, ladies. We've wasted enough time as it is.'

Jade proved to be an Olympic-style skater. She glowed with new confidence by the time we'd finished. Gloria had her own innovative style and managed to remain upright. I took to it like a duck to skates, breaking six plates before pulling a table down on top of me. Donny and a builder rushed upstairs, and Tracy told me I was useless and had better shape up.

Bambi on Ice

A week later, with Tracy's caustic comments still ringing in my ears, I stood at the entrance to the police station with trembling knees. Putting a hand down to steady them, I winced at the ugly bruises showing through my sparkly tights.

One officer placed a hand on my arm. 'C'mon, Miss. Let's get you in.'

As I moved forward, the tall one exclaimed, 'Bloody hell, it's like Bambi on ice.'

They both grabbed an arm and transported me to the desk without a skate hitting the ground.

The custody sergeant looked up from his paperwork and smiled. The corners of his soft brown eyes crinkled before the professional mask came down. He had a nice dad-type face. The sort of dad I'd have liked to pick me up from school, teach me to drive, that sort of thing. He read out a heap of information I couldn't take in. Something about my rights and free legal advice. I hoped I said 'thanks' in all the right places. At one stage, his voice softened, and he asked if I understood why I was there.

I gulped. 'Suspicion of murder.'

A crease appeared between his brows.

'I know. Isn't that ridiculous when I don't actually know who's died?'

The crease deepened.

'You see, I didn't even notice the body. Not at first, anyway. And then I was too shocked to take a proper look. I just remember the blood.'

He leaned over the desk to view my skates. 'You'd better remove those. Take these.' He handed me a cellophane-wrapped pair of sauna-type slippers. 'I'll give you a receipt for the skates.'

'It's all right. You can chuck 'em in the canal for all I care.' And just so he didn't think I was wasteful as well as a murderer, I added, 'They're a death trap.' Probably not the best thing to say.

'Can I inform anyone you're here, Ms Merang?'

I stared as if he'd asked if I could fly.

'Boyfriend, husband, parents?' From the despairing look in his eye, I thought he was going to add 'carer'.

A sob rose in my throat. 'I don't have any of those. Well, I've got a husband, but he doesn't love me any more, and I don't even know where he is.'

His face remained impassive. 'Mmm, I see. Perhaps a—'

'Friend.' I pounced on the word. 'Yes, I've got a friend. James. He lives in London,' I tagged on the end as if it had any relevance.

'Can you give me his number?'

I scribbled it on the sheet. 'James. We've been best friends since we were five.' A surge of relief ran through me. My world might have caved in, but I'd always have James.

The sergeant drummed his fingers on the desk as he waited for James to answer. Scared he might not pick up, I buried my face in my hands until the sergeant cleared his throat and began explaining my predicament.

'Yes, sir. I'm sure it's a shock.' He held the phone from his ear as expletives rang around the room. 'Yes, sir. I'll tell her that.' The officer replaced the receiver and smiled. 'He says not to worry. He'll get you the best solicitor in Leeds and not to answer any questions from the bastards in the meantime.'

'Oh, sorry about that. He won't have realised what he was saying.'

'Don't worry, love. We've heard all the usual endearments. Now let's get you into one of our suites.' Clocking my goose-pimpled arms, he added, 'I'll get you a blanket.' He nodded to the officers. 'Do all the necessaries and put her in number four.'

They led me down a grey corridor. The oversized footwear made my feet slap the floor like a tired old clown's. First, they showed me into a small room where an unsmiling female officer swabbed inside my mouth and took fingerprints. Then we set off again.

The spartan cell wasn't too bad. The door banged behind me, but an officer then opened the hatch and promised a cup of tea. I sat on the blue padded bench and put my head in my hands.

A cold and lonely police cell was the ideal place for self-recrimination. I'd no one to blame but myself. Why did I take the first catering job offered? Then, on the back of it, I rushed to the nearest estate agent's and accepted a grubby bedsit in a shared house.

I'd cast myself as a broken-hearted heroine, indifferent to her surroundings. What a conceit. Two weeks in, and the foul entrance hall, rat droppings, and perpetual parties of the girl downstairs had got to me.

Apart from the bars at the window, the cell was an improvement. The only thing missing was the globe on my bedside table, which I liked to spin each night and wonder where Zack might be. Would my globe-trotting husband still call me boring, now I'd been arrested for murder?

'Hels,' he'd said just before he left. 'You're too content being the happy homemaker. I want more out of life.'

It was too late to say I wanted that too. Happy as a pig in mud in our docker's cottage, I'd failed to realise Zack's priorities might differ from mine. Having lived under Prue's regime since the age of fourteen, I'd wanted to create a warm, happy home.

Thinking of Prue made me burst into tears. As a surrogate mum, she'd always done her best for me, and I'd wanted to make her proud. After this, she'd never be able to hold her head up in Buttersley again.

Once they'd started, the tears wouldn't stop, and the reality of my situation hit home. What if they charged me and sent me to prison on remand? I'd be tried for murder and maybe locked up forever.

Shivering, I pulled the blanket around me. I needed to banish those fears and stay positive. When I got out, I'd visit Prue and tell her my plans. Working at Donny's Doughnuts had been a stepping stone towards my dream. A means of gaining relevant experience. Whatever the outcome, I couldn't go back there. For one thing, there was a killer on the loose. It could have been anyone at Donny's grand opening. Whoever it was must be pretty pleased they'd pinned it on me.

It could only help to go through the events of the previous evening. I might remember something significant that would point to the real murderer. But perhaps I needed to go back even further. The tensions at Donny's had been there from the start.

I jumped when someone slid back the hatch of my cell door. 'Cup of tea.'

I'd usually turn up my nose at tea in polystyrene, but it tasted pretty good. The officer even promised a microwave meal at twelve. I had no idea of the time.

Sipping my drink, I recalled that first training session at Donny's after we'd tried on our uniforms. I picked up the retail aspects easily enough and could rattle off the doughnut flavours in no time, but it first got sticky around the allergens debate.

Tracy had handed us reams of printed paper. 'You need to memorise all these ingredients and allergens.'

Gloria pretended to sink under the weight of the sheets. 'I'll never get through all this.'

Tracy held up her pudgy palm. 'Not now. Read it in your own time.'

Narrowing her eyes, Gloria perused the first sheet. 'Just to get us on the right track, Tracy, if I were a lacto-intolerant vegetarian, which doughnut would you recommend?'

Tracy pursed her lips. 'I—'

'Bearing in mind, I don't do sulphites.'

Tracy's scowl fused her top lip to her nose. I had a flashback to my turbulent teenage years. Prue used to say, "If the wind changes, your face will stay like that". Perhaps Tracy needed to know that.

The door opened, and Tracy's grimace turned into a smile. 'Da—Donny, we were just discussing the allergens.'

'Ladies, ladies.' Donny strutted towards us. 'You don't need to worry about that boring stuff. My doughnuts couldn't harm anyone. Full of natural goodness, they are.'

'And E numbers,' said Jade under her breath. 'Pretty stratospheric levels, actually.'

'That's another thing for us to discuss, Donald,' said Pauline at his side. 'We need to be fully compliant.' She turned to the tall, middle-aged man in a pinstripe who'd followed them in. 'Graham would back me on that.'

The man nodded his grey quiff, and miniature snowflakes drifted onto his shoulders. 'Absolutely, Pauline. I'm with *you* on that. You can't risk being sued.'

Donny's moustache quivered, and his cheeks burned a deep shade of red. Through rigid lips, he mimicked the other man's voice. 'I'm with *you* on that.'

Pauline glared at her husband. 'Donald, that's—'

'Don't start. It's my shop. I'll do and say what I want.' Donny pointed at them both. 'You two should have stayed together. You could have bored each other to death.'

I pulled a 'what's-going-on-face' at Gloria. She raised her eyebrows and flicked her head at Tracy, who was staring hard at the group. Fists clenched at her side, she looked ready to pounce.

Stepping up to Graham, Donny waved a fat finger in his face. 'Why don't you eff-off with your abacus and leave me to run the business.'

Almost a foot taller, Graham loomed over Donny. 'You've always been a little sh—'

Pauline inserted herself between them. 'Gentleman, please. Let's be professional here.'

After a final challenging glare, Donny pulled back his shoulders. Graham stepped away with a dazed expression and smoothed down his hair.

'Can we get on now?' said Tracy. 'My team is waiting for your approval.'

'What?' Graham jerked his head and started another mini avalanche. He stared in our direction as if only just noticing our presence.

Tracy nudged him. 'Do you like the uniforms? I designed them myself.'

Graham examined us like bugs under a microscope. Jade trembled, Gloria swore under her breath, and I sweated profusely in my polyester fibres. A smile twitched on his lips. 'Tracy, my dear, you've surpassed yourself.'

Pauline cleared her throat as if she wanted to test out her voice. 'How's the skating going?' She turned to Graham. 'As you know, I have—'

'Great,' said Tracy. 'We'll give you a demonstration. Sit down, and Gloria and Jade will pretend to serve you.' She seized my arm and pulled me aside. 'Don't dare move. You'll ruin it all.'

Jade glided with the speed of a gazelle. She could even skate backwards. Gloria's style was sporadic, more monkey-style than gazelle, but she could shift pretty quickly.

Donny clapped and whistled. 'I knew it would work. Look at 'em go.' His buoyancy had returned in full. 'What with my delicious doughnuts, these lovely ladies, and Tracy in charge, we can't fail.'

At five, Tracy clapped her hands. 'Right, ladies. I'm calling it a wrap. Report for your first proper shift on Monday.'

'Will the builders have finished by then?' asked Jade.

'Yes. You'll have three days to clean and set the shop up before our soft opening on Thursday. Don't wear your uniforms till then. I don't want 'em getting mucked up.'

'Oh, I was going to go shopping in mine,' said Gloria. 'What's a soft opening?'

'Special invitees only. Treat them as real customers. Our grand opening party is on Friday evening. You'll have to stay late for that, and then we open properly on Saturday.'

'I'm going to have one last skate around,' I said.

Five minutes later, I gave the thumbs up to Gloria. I'd finally cracked it. My feet seemed to know where to go, and I was just thinking of increasing my speed when the door opened and threw me off balance. I collided with a young, wiry man with gelled-back hair.

'Hey-up, love. Where you off to in such a hurry?'

I recoiled from his grey, grubby tracksuit. 'Sorry, sorry. Hope you're not—'

'No harm done.' His gaze ran over my body, and he licked his thin lips. 'Hey, darlin', you can throw yourself at me anytime.'

Gloria made her choking prawn noise, but she was drowned out by Tracy bellowing 'R-y-a-n.'

Before he sauntered over to Tracy, Ryan winked at me. 'See ya later, darlin'.'

'You're dismissed for today.' Tracy patted Jade on the back. 'You've done very well.' She hesitated a moment and then did the same to Gloria before turning her back on me. 'C'mon, ladies. Grab your belongings. Quick as you can. My fiancé's taking me out for a meal.'

As we headed towards the door, Gloria whispered. 'Don't fancy what either of 'em's got for afters. Who's up for a quick drink? I certainly need one.'

Ampsley Jail Beckons

In my police cell, I pushed the plastic plate of congealed pasta away and put my hands over my ears. Earlier, I'd been oblivious to the noise made by my fellow prisoners, but now their shouts, bangs, and thuds set me on edge. As the shock of my arrest dwindled, the implications nibbled away at me like a pack of hungry rats.

Staring at the pasta, I couldn't escape the sweaty cheese smell that filled the room. Could it be just one week ago, that Saturday after our first training session – when drunk on cheap wine, I'd devoured a bowl of carbonara at the cosy Italian and shared stories with my new best friends? I thought back to that night and smiled.

We'd downed two bottles of prosecco at the wine bar before moving on to the restaurant. By then, Jade had lost her paleness, and two rosy circles danced on her cheeks. As for Gloria, she fizzed and sparkled like a seaside arcade. Sitting at her side, I glowed in her reflected rays, and a bolt of optimism surged through me. I would achieve my dream of having my own shop and tea room. Anything was possible.

I held up my glass. 'Here's to Donny's greasy doughnuts. I'm so pleased to have met you both.'

'Here's to us wheelies,' said Gloria.

I groaned. 'Don't remind me. I'm covered in bruises. I'm going to practise in the park tomorrow.'

Gloria cut into her meat feast pizza. 'Which park is that? Where do you live?'

'Ampsley. Near the jail.'

'What?' Gloria widened her striking blue eyes. 'I had you down as a posh bird. You're not from round here.'

What would Zack say to that? He used to joke he'd got himself a "rough bit of stuff". At least I *thought* he was joking until he hinted I should polish myself up a bit when we started our corporate life.

'That's where you're wrong, Gloria. I'm from Buttersley. I left when I was eighteen to go to Liverpool uni. Then I worked in London.'

'That sounds exciting,' said Jade.

Keen to move the subject away from me, I asked if she was a student.

'In my second year.'

I studied her earnest expression. Big, dark eyes shone out from a smooth, unblemished surface. How could I have thought her plain?

With a pang, I realised I must have been the same age when I met Zack. Had we looked as young as that? That was no age to meet your life partner. No wonder he took off when he did.

'Have you got a boyfriend, love?' Gloria asked Jade as she topped up our glasses.

Jade picked at a bread roll. 'Sort of. He's on my course.'

'Well, don't bloody marry him.' My voice rang out louder than intended. Customers at other tables turned their heads.

Gloria laughed. 'There speaks a bitter woman. But Helen's right. Spread your love around. Don't get tied down.'

Jade took a healthy swig of her wine.

I raised my glass again. 'From one bitter woman to another, Gloria. What happened to you?'

'What?' Gloria's fork fell to the floor, and she dived to retrieve it. When she resurfaced, the unexpected hint of tears told me to change the subject.

'Zack – my husband – left me because I was boring,' I blurted out.

'He obviously hasn't seen you on roller skates, love,' said Gloria, her eyes sparkling once more. 'I could watch you all day.'

'Don't.' Jade giggled. 'Oh, Helen, when you pulled that table down on top of yourself, I thought Tracy—'

'Was going to wet herself,' finished Gloria. 'She probably did, which is why she had that pained look on her face all afternoon. Seriously, Helen, how could you ever be boring?'

I smiled. 'Thanks. That means a lot.'

'Zack will be back,' Gloria said. 'I absolutely guarantee. It won't be tomorrow, maybe not even this year, but he'll crawl back sometime, begging for your forgiveness.' She spoke with such conviction that my heart did a hopeful skip and a hop.

I was just about to reply when Jade slapped her palms onto the table and stood. 'But you will say ...' She took a large gulp of wine and swayed. 'You will say, "Sorry, Zack, you're too late. I'm now Mrs Donoghue-Doughnut the fourth".' Falling back into her seat, she added, 'Think I'm going to be sick.'

Gloria jumped up and heaved the girl to her feet. 'We'll leave Helen to plan her wedding to Donny.'

As they tottered away, I closed my eyes and possibly nodded off. I started when a hand bounced on my head. 'Hey, sleepy. We're back.' Jade put her face up close to mine. Her dark eyes were bigger than ever. 'Ready to party?'

'Let's have some water first,' I said.

She flopped back onto her seat and giggled. 'Only if you let me be your bridesmaid when you marry Donny.'

Gloria winked. 'He might be back on the market soon. He doesn't seem to be getting on well with Pauline.'

Jade's head slumped to one side. 'You're much nicer than her, Helen, with your lovely green eyes and bouncy curls.' She laid her head on the table. 'I'm going to sleep now. Night night.'

'Sleep tight, little one,' said Gloria. We smiled at each other over her head.

'Pauline seems pretty friendly with Graham and his dandruff,' I said. 'What's his position? How does he fit in?'

'Donny said something about an abacus. So, putting two and two together as Graham might do all day, he's possibly Donny's accountant?'

'My God. Nothing gets past you.'

'That's what my husband used to say.'

Used to say? 'Are you divorced?'

Gloria twiddled the stem of her glass. 'Widowed. Harry died four years ago when the twins were fourteen.'

'Fourteen, just like ...' I'd been about to say, the same age as me when my mum died, but it wasn't about me. 'It's tough at that age as it is.'

'I know.' A single tear sprang from Gloria's brimming eyes. I squeezed her hand.

She wiped away the tear. 'The last four years I've concentrated on the boys, but they don't need me now. I thought it was time to get back out there.'

'And the world of Donny's Doughnuts is your springboard.'

The light returned to her eyes. 'What was I thinking? But it'll be a laugh, won't it? Something we probably both need.'

'Though I don't know how long I can put up with Tracy.'

'She does seem to have it in for you. But she's the type that has to pick on someone to make herself feel good. She can't find fault with superstar Jade, and she's scared of me, so you're the obvious choice.' Gloria pleated her napkin. 'I actually feel sorry for her. She puts on that act because she's out of her depth. She hasn't a clue what she's doing.'

'At least Donny thinks she's marvellous.'

She snorted. 'Him? The only person he's interested in is himself. He gets everyone to do his dirty work, while he bustles around with that false *bonhomie*.' Gloria yawned. 'Get me with my fancy words. I suppose it's time to go. I'll wake Tinker Bell.'

We stood in a tired huddle outside the restaurant while the Saturday night revellers swarmed all around us. Gloria had her arm around Jade, who seemed asleep on her feet.

'Jade lives near me,' she said. 'We'll get a taxi together, and I'll make sure she gets home. But let's put you in one first.'

'It's okay. I'll walk.'

A note of sharpness entered her voice. 'Don't be ridiculous. You can't walk home at this time, not to where *you* live near that prison.'

Ampsley Jail. The estate agent hadn't mentioned I'd be living on its doorstep. Horror stories of the castellated monolith had reached even the playgrounds of Buttersley.

'That's where they hang naughty girls like you,' James – my so-called friend – used to say whenever I got into trouble.

A Harbinger Thingy

The next time an officer slid back the hatch, I bolted from the bench. 'Can you tell me how long I've been here, please? And has my solicitor arrived?'

'No, sorry.'

If I'd been behind actual bars, I might have rattled them. 'Is that the answer to both my questions?'

'I need to get on. You'll be the first to know.'

The hatch banged shut. The first to know. He'd made it sound like I was asking who'd won *The X Factor*. How long could they keep me there? Surely, I had rights? What about prison reform? Why hadn't the police found the real culprit? They'd been quick enough to arrest me. It must have been obvious by then that I wasn't a murderer. I suddenly went cold. What if they weren't looking for anyone else? They could be jamming the evidence together like a child with a jigsaw.

If only I'd seen the body first. *I'd* have been the one to alert the police. My actions would have seemed natural. It didn't seem plausible – even to me – that I'd not noticed it lying there. Then again, they'd not seen me on skates.

On the Monday leading up to our grand opening, Gloria had grabbed my arm as I skidded past. 'Helen, you're like a demon in blinkers. You need to be aware of what's around you. Otherwise, you'll be knocking kids down like skittles.'

Jade retrieved the chair I'd sent flying. 'Try relaxing your legs.'

'And your jaw,' said Gloria. 'That scowl will finish off any kids left standing. And don't clench your teeth.'

'Easier said than done,' I called over my shoulder as I rolled down the length of the chequered tiles before coming up against a soft, squidgy wall.

Tracy stiffened. 'Get off me, you bloody idiot.'

'Sorry, sorry. Didn't see you there.'

'Take those skates off now. You don't need them on when we're setting up.' Tracy smoothed down her navy blue business suit. 'Practise in your own time and remember, you're on a trial period.'

At the end of the day, Tracy made an executive decision. 'You,' she prodded my front, 'will stay behind the counter where you can do the least damage. The other two will serve the tables.'

That suited me. The counter ran almost the length of the diner. I'd have plenty of things to grab for support.

'You'll be the link between the servers and Donny in the kitchen.' Tracy inclined her head to the closed door behind the counter. 'You'll communicate with him through the hatch and call him Chef. Do not under any circumstances enter when he's working. Your only purpose in there is to clean after he's left the building.'

'Okay.'

Tracy fixed her beady eyes upon me as if she were expecting more of a response.

'Boss,' I threw in for good measure.

That did the trick, and she returned to running a candy-pink nail down her checklist.

I loved having my own territory behind the mint-green Formica counter. Once the diner opened to customers, I'd engage with the regulars as they perched on the red-topped stools. They'd marvel at my milkshakes and admire the froth on my coffee while I made it all look so easy.

On Tuesday, Donny arrived as I was stacking the cups on top of the coffee machine. He bustled into the kitchen and closed the door.

I stuck my head through the hatch. 'Morning, Chef. Would you like a coffee?'

Stroking his moustache as if it were a pet, his eyes remained fixed on a mountain of steel equipment. 'No thanks. I need to get to grips with this hot dog steamer.'

'Okay, Chef. I'll leave you to it.'

With 'Jailhouse Rock' on repeat, the others possibly didn't hear the clatter and frustrated cries coming from the kitchen.

When smoke billowed out through the hatch, I yelled, 'Tracy.' She didn't look up from her phone. 'Boss.'

'What do you want?'

'Donny might need a hand.'

She dropped her phone. 'Oh, my God. Do something, will you? Get in there now.'

I could have said I wasn't allowed, but after clamping a wet tea towel to my face, I yanked open the door. Through the smoke and steam, Donny's prostrate body loomed like a beached mini whale. I dropped to my knees and dragged him out by his ankles just as the fire alarm went crazy. Jade rushed in with the fire blanket. Tracy burst into tears.

'No harm done,' said Donny when he'd coughed and spluttered back to life.

United in shock, we all sat together at a table by the window. Tracy had not yet recovered. Vivid, ugly blotches had sprouted on her cheeks, and rivulets of mascara snaked down to her chin. White, shaking knuckles clung to the clipboard as if it were all she had in the world, and her eyes remained fixed on Donny.

'You can't get rid of me that easily,' he joked, but his limp moustache matched the wet strands of hair on either side of his bald patch, and his smile seemed forced. 'And no, Tracy, my love, I don't need a doctor.'

I'd made us all cappuccinos. Never mind my daring rescue, I was miffed when no one commented on the height of my froth.

'Perhaps you should leave it for today, Da—Donny,' said Tracy. 'I'll make sure Helen deep cleans the kitchen so it'll be all sparkling for you tomorrow.'

He placed his hand on hers. 'Okey-dokey, my little pink petal. Yes, I'll do that. I need to fine-tune my doughnut toppings, anyway. No rest for the wicked, hey?' He chuckled as if he'd said something funny. 'I'll hit you with my hot dogs tomorrow.'

Gloria sighed. 'Oh, what a shame. I'm a vegetarian.'

'So am I,' said Jade, a little too quickly.

Donny patted my arm and beamed at me as if I'd won the rollover jackpot. 'Helen, my dear, aren't you the lucky one?'

When an officer delivered my second meal to the cell, I realised it must be late afternoon or maybe evening already. In that false cocoon, I had no idea. I poked at the sausage and beans, and although it looked more appetising than Donny's flaccid hot dogs, I pushed it away and reached for the tea.

Recalling Donny lying flat-out in the kitchen had focused my thoughts. For the first time, a general outline of the dead body came to mind. It had been a man lying there – possibly Donny! I gasped. Perhaps the fire incident had been one of those thingies. What was the word? Harbinger – that was it. I clutched my blanket – a harbinger of his own death? But who would have wanted to kill him, and how would they have managed it unobserved?

Hot to Trot

Sipping my tea in the cell, I realised it couldn't have been Donny lying dead in the kitchen – not from Tracy's reactions. She'd calmly told me to put the knife down, led me away, and rang the police. If it had been him, she'd have gone to pieces. The victim had to be someone she didn't care about. So that must also rule out her boyfriend. Unless sleazeball Ryan had finally pushed her too far.

The events leading up to the murder continued to play in my head. On Thursday, the day before the party, Ryan rocked up with all the swagger of Billy the Kid. Pecking Tracy's cheek, he cast his eyes around the diner as if weighing up the cost.

Tracy grabbed his hand. 'What d'you think, babe?'

He sucked through his teeth. 'A bit flash if you ask me. All this chrome. Donny must have more money than sense.'

'Sit here, hun. I'll get Gloria to serve you.'

'I'll sit at the counter. That other one can see to me.'

I kept my head down at the sink to hide my distaste.

'Hello, darlin'. We meet again.'

Raising my eyes, I caught Ryan leering down my top. Unsmiling, I handed him a menu.

He tossed it back onto the bar. 'I don't want none of them gay-looking doughnuts. What can you offer a real man?'

'The hot dogs are excellent,' I lied. 'Especially with the Hot-to-Trot mustard.' A good dollop of that would sort him out.

'Okay. Get me two.' He puffed out his chest. 'I've got a stonkin' appetite. Can't get enough. Know what I mean?'

Gloria whizzed past, a stack of menus under one arm. She pointed at Ryan and pretended to gag.

'And what can I get you to drink?' I asked.

'Coke. Make it extra large, seeing as it's on the house.'

'It's not.'

'What?'

'On the house. It's a soft opening day. Everything's half price.'

He shrugged. 'Tracy'll pay for mine.' Licking his reedy lips, he leaned in to whisper, 'What I want to know is, how's *your* soft opening?'

I spilt the contents of the ice bucket into his lap. 'Oops! Sorry about that, Ryan.'

Like a blowfly homing in on a corpse, Tracy appeared with a towel. 'Helen, you're so bloody clumsy.'

Donny poked his head out of the hatch. His red face glistened with sweat. 'Tracy, love, can you help me out here? Having a spot of bother with the toastie thingy.'

She handed Ryan the towel. 'Back in a sec, babe.'

But Ryan had a long wait. He wasn't the only one. The diner had filled with noisy, hungry customers. Gloria and Jade zoomed around like whirligigs, and I made endless milkshakes and coffees. The food orders piled up, but only a banging noise came out of the kitchen.

Standing behind the counter, the customers seemed to think I was in charge, and they didn't hold back with their complaints. I nearly rolled out of the place there and then.

Loud noises outside my police cell brought me back to the present. Drunken voices shouted and swore. Could it be Saturday night already? Where the hell was my solicitor? I thought back to those impatient diners. They should try waiting for legal representation. It was a lot more stressful than hanging about for a mouldy old hot dog.

'Your solicitor's stuck in traffic,' said the officer who delivered the next drink. 'We could call the duty one for you?'

I was tempted to accept, but James had hired his hotshot solicitor, and I didn't want to let him down.

I lay on the hard bench and closed my eyes. Comfort-wise, it was on a par with the banana crate back at my bedsit. When the money came through from the sale of our cottage and the apartment, I planned to buy a small house in Buttersley and launch my business. That would make the split from Zack all the more real.

It took Pauline to sort out the diner. After arriving with Graham, she rushed into the kitchen. A moment later, she stuck her head out of the hatch. 'Give me five minutes, and I'll start getting those orders out. Tell the others.'

I released a deep breath in relief.

Graham stood at the end of the counter where Pauline had left him. His drab brown suit, beige shirt, and thin tie didn't do him any favours.

I passed him a one-shot Americano. 'I understand you're Donny's accountant?'

'Yes.' He stirred his coffee.

'So you'll be coming to the party tomorrow evening?'

He nodded and ran a hand through his hair.

As the particles drifted, I made a mental note to give the counter a thorough wipe when he left. 'Pauline seems to be sorting out the problem in the kitchen.'

'She's very capable.' He withdrew a magazine from his briefcase, spread it out on the counter, and turned his full attention to 'Systems Analytics'.

At closing time, Tracy gathered us together for a debriefing. Pauline said she couldn't stay as she had an appointment elsewhere. I'd already poked my head around the kitchen door expecting chaos, but she'd left it immaculately clean, with the appliances all shiny and ready for action.

Tracy consulted her clipboard. 'Gloria and Jade, you've totally nailed those skates. Helen, what can I say?' She gave a resigned shake of her head. 'You're still not getting it. You can't hide behind that counter all the time chatting up the men. When the other two are busy, I need you out there, clearing the tables.'

'I thought you wanted me to stay—'

'Raise any issues with me privately.'

Donny patted my arm. 'You'll get there eventually, my dear. Even I started small.'

'What went wrong in the kitchen?' asked Gloria.

The Donoghues exchanged a glance. 'Nothing serious,' said Tracy. 'Just a minor malfunction with a piece of equipment.'

Donny opened his arms. 'Then I had to show Pauline the ropes, so I can have a day off now and again. But tell me, ladies, what did everyone think of the food?'

Reflecting on what I'd shoved in the bin, I shuddered. The hot dogs had come back like dissected worms, with hardened globules of cheese clinging like barnacles.

'The kids loved the sparkles on the doughnuts,' said Jade.

Donny cocked his head. 'And—'

'Everyone loved it,' said Tracy in a firm voice. 'They said it was ... it was ... gourmet.'

I marvelled at her invention, while Gloria did her choking noise thing again.

After Tracy dismissed us, I suggested a drink at the wine bar.

'Oh, I'd love to,' said Jade, 'but I'm meeting my boyfriend.'

'And the boys are cooking my tea,' said Gloria. 'Which is a first. Another time?'

I smiled to hide my disappointment. 'Yeah, sure. Have a great time, both of you. See you tomorrow.'

Walking quickly through the city centre, I couldn't avoid glancing into the brightly lit bars with their Thursday night crowd. Men with loosened ties and pints in both hands stood in jostling groups. The women had discarded their smart jackets to reveal see-through blouses, and no doubt they were gossiping about the latest office affair. It all looked so inviting. I'd kill to be there with a double gin and tonic. Instead, I called in at the mini-mart for a frozen meal for one.

A Dead Dark Horse

The anaemic bolognaise I chose from the mini-mart was exactly the same as the first meal served in my police cell. I was contemplating the coincidence and the mysteries of time when someone slid back the hatch.

'Your solicitor's here.' As the officer led me, I anticipated the type of solicitor James might engage: a wise, avuncular man in tweeds who would speak in measured tones and know the law inside out. Or perhaps a young blade in a flashy suit, who'd have a loud voice and shoot from the hip.

'Helen, lovely to meet you. I'm Leticia Manning.' The statuesque, flaxen-haired beauty held out a strong, capable hand. 'So sorry about your wait. I've had the journey from hell, but that's enough about me. How are you bearing up?'

'A bit bewildered, I suppose.'

'James sounded distraught. I've never known him to lose his cool like that.'

'You know him well?'

Her dazzling smile faltered. 'We briefly went out together at university.'

'Oh, I think he mentioned you,' I lied. There had been so many.

'Did he?' Her voice rose, and two spots of pink appeared on her smooth, pearly cheeks. 'I was perhaps a little too county-set for him.' She suddenly grinned. 'I wore pearls, for heaven's sake. He left me for a vixen in a boob tube. No hard feelings, though. And you and James? Did you ever? I mean, are you—'

'Strictly platonic. More like brother and sister.'

'I see. That's lovely.' She opened her notebook. 'Right. Let's get down to business and get you out of here. The police have given me full disclosure. It's a very flimsy case, I must say. The poor lambs don't have a leg to stand on. They've gathered more evidence since your arrest, and my delay has actually worked in our favour.'

She'd already put me at ease, and now I almost wept with relief. 'All I did, Leticia, was pick up a stained knife. I thought someone had chucked it in the sink at last night's party. Donny had a big cake, you see. He cut it and gave us all a piece. When I saw the knife in the sink the next morning, I thought it was covered in dried jam.'

She scrawled her notes with a confident hand. 'Yes, dried jam – or rather blood – that fits with the estimated time of death. The victim had been dead for some hours. So you picked up a knife, but what about the body on the floor?'

I took a deep breath. 'I didn't notice it at first. From the kitchen door, it wasn't in my line of vision. It lay to the side of the sink.'

A crease appeared between her brows. 'I see,' she said in a tone suggesting she didn't.

'I wanted to check the sink was all clean for Donny. And the thing is, because I'm so useless on skates, I had to focus on where I was going. So, from the kitchen door, I concentrated on the sink and launched myself at it. I only noticed the body when Tracy pointed it out.'

The crease lifted slightly. 'Okay. I'll have to think about that.'

'And even when I saw the body, it didn't register. Must have been the shock. I still don't know who's died.'

'A Mr Graham Sutty.'

I squealed.

'Ah, did you know him?'

'Vaguely. He's ... He was Donny's accountant.' The shock made me stammer. 'He caused a stir at the opening party on Friday night.'

Leticia leaned forward. 'That sounds interesting. Can you elaborate?'

I thought back to Graham's entrance at the party.

'Bloody hell. Graham's a dark horse.' Gloria spun a full circle with a plateful of doughnuts in one hand. 'He's just walked in. Check out the eye candy dangling from his arm.'

Jade steered backwards in a perfectly straight line. 'Looks like a Kardashian. What's she doing with such an old man?'

Desperately grabbing a chair for support, I swivelled to face them. 'Her boobs are like balloons!' I hadn't meant to shout. Several heads turned.

Pauline's glass fell from her hand and smashed on the hard, chequered tiles. 'Graham, how *could* you?'

She ran from the room in her sensible brown shoes. I wanted to go after her. She'd been almost kind in my interview, but it was a long way to skate, and I didn't have the nerve in front of a crowd. I retreated behind the counter.

Tracy turned up the jukebox. The hum of conversation started again, but all eyes remained on Graham and his companion. With his hand at the small of her back, they headed towards my counter.

'Good evening,' I said. 'What can I get you to drink?'

Graham turned to the girl. 'Tia-Marie?'

I was just about to say we didn't serve liqueurs, when Ryan, of all people, saved me.

He tapped her arm. 'You didn't call yourself that fancy name when we were at school.'

She ignored him and gave me a pleasant smile. 'Just water, thanks.'

'And you didn't have those melons then, love, or all that hair. Bet the whole lot's fake.'

Tia-Marie gazed serenely over the top of Ryan's head. Only a delicate twitch of her nostrils indicated an unpleasant smell below.

Graham bristled. 'Ryan, why don't you go and be annoying somewhere else?'

'Hey, old man, don't tell *me* what to do.' Ryan squared up to Graham. A large, fake-gold watch dangled down an arm, and convict-style jeans hung low on his scrawny behind.

Tracy appeared like a bloodhound. 'Everything okay, babe?' She ran her hand down Ryan's back. 'There's someone over there who's dying to meet you.'

'I can't believe that,' Gloria said from the side of her mouth as she whirled past.

As Tracy led Ryan away, she called over her shoulder. 'Helen, why haven't you got Graham and his *friend* a drink yet?'

'I'll have a large whisky,' said Graham, his face grim. 'In fact, just leave me the bottle.'

After I'd served them, I washed a stack of glasses and couldn't help overhearing their conversation. Graham droned on about his problems with audits. Holding her head on one side, Tia-Marie puckered her brow, as if such difficulties were the bane of her life.

Though dominating the exchange, Graham still managed to throw back the whisky. Eventually, they seemed to realise they had something in common, and Tia-Marie spoke with increased animation.

Donny strode towards them with a dark look of intent. 'Good evening, Tia-Marie. I didn't know you were a *friend* of Graham's.'

She pecked him on the cheek.

'Actually,' said Graham, 'Tia-Marie's been telling me something about you.'

Donny smiled, but it wasn't his usual beam, and his fingers twitched at his moustache. 'All good, I hope?' He forced out a laugh. Casting around, he held out his hand, and Jade glided to a halt.

'Jade, my dear, could you give Tia-Marie a tour of the diner? Show her our memorabilia.'

Raising her brow at me, Jade said, 'Of course.'

As soon as the women had gone, and I'd moved a discreet distance away, Donny held his finger up to Graham's face. 'Listen, mate. I know your game.'

Graham swatted the finger away. 'Let's get this straight. I've never been your mate. Your accountant and ex-brother-in-law, yes. A mate, no.'

'Why did you bother to come then on my big night?'

'Pauline invited me.'

'She didn't ask you to bring that piece of trash. Look how it's upset her.'

'From what Tia-Marie tells me, you're not above a bit of trash, yourself.'

After a quick look over his shoulder, Donny lowered his voice, and I missed the next bit.

Graham didn't seem to have such reservations. The jukebox juddered to a halt, and anyone could have heard his next words. 'Tia-Marie's told me about you and Liz, which confirms what I've suspected all along.'

Gloria plonked a pile of dirty glasses in front of me. 'Who the hell's Liz?'

After the confrontation, Donny strutted off, and Graham glugged from his glass as if it contained life-saving medicine. Then, shaking his head, he took a small notebook from his inside pocket. As he wrote, flakes of scurf tumbled onto my counter, and I crushed a cloth in my frustrated desire to get at it.

Replacing the notebook, he glanced around the diner and raised his glass at Tia-Marie, who was standing at the jukebox with Jade. She didn't seem in any hurry to return.

Pauline brushed past her, perhaps heading towards us. But as Graham hunched over the counter, it was Tracy who tapped his shoulder.

'How could you upset my dad on his big night? This diner's his dream. Don't you realise how much it all means?' Livid scarlet blotches had broken out on her chest.

'Tracy love, I didn't mean—'

'And why have you brought that woman? Pauline's upset.'

Graham whipped up his head, and I dreaded to think of the fallout. 'Since when have you been bothered about Pauline? You seem to despise her as much as you did our Liz.'

Gloria came to a halt and leaned on the counter. 'God, I'm knackered, and these skates have given me a blister.' She lowered her voice. 'Hey, what's going on with Tracy and old snowstorm head?'

I put a finger to my lips. 'Listen.'

'Your precious sister, Graham, was out for what she could get. She took my dad for a ride.'

He stood, and a vein bulged at his temple. 'I think you'll find, my dear, it was the other way around. And from what I've heard tonight, there are questions I need—'

'At least women find my dad attractive.' She jabbed at his chest. 'He doesn't have to pay for it. She should be charging you double, you ugly old letch.'

I cringed. 'Brutal.'

Gloria stared open-mouthed. 'Bloody hell. Look out, his date's coming back.'

Closing my eyes, I clamped both hands over my ears. 'I can't witness any more.' Hearing nothing, I whispered, 'What's going on?'

'Tia-Marie's saying something to Tracy. Can't make it out. Tracy's stormed off. You can open your eyes now. Hey, Jade, did you catch what Tia-Marie said when you flashed past?'

Jade executed a textbook stop. 'Yeah, it was something like, "You might want to tell Ryan he can't afford me".'

Graham and Tia-Marie remained at the counter. Him knocking back the whisky and her sipping water. Despite her efforts to engage him, Graham barely responded. He seemed to have something on his mind.

A Clapped-Out Cheerleader

I sat back on the hard chair and gazed at Leticia across the chipped table. I'd rambled on about Donny's party for ages. With all that talking, I could have done with a cup of tea.

As Leticia twiddled her pen, the stark light bounced off her shell-pink nails. 'You're building up a brilliant picture. It will all help with your defence.'

'Will I have to tell the police all about the party?'

'It depends on what they ask. When they interview you, answer their questions as briefly as possible. Don't elaborate, don't explain.'

I swallowed. 'You mean they'll try to trick me?'

'Don't think of it like that. They're just doing their job, which, unfortunately, is to make you incriminate yourself.' She gave a reassuring smile. 'But we both know that's impossible, as—'

'I didn't do it.'

'Exactly. And I'll be sitting right beside you. So if I don't want you to answer a particular question, I'll tap you on the knee, and you'll say, "No comment". Got that?'

I attempted a smile. Could this be happening? Alone in the cell for so long, I'd become detached from the harsh reality of my situation. I'd clung to the hope that the police would come to their senses, apologise and release me with their heartfelt best wishes.

'Don't be daunted by the formality of the interview,' Leticia continued. 'It will be under caution, which just means they'll make that statement you hear on police dramas. "You do not have to say anything, but it may harm your defence" blah de blah. All pretty standard stuff. Nothing to worry about.'

Despite her reassurances, my legs were shaking, and as I clamped sweaty hands on my knees, bile rose in my throat. 'They're never going to believe I didn't notice a dead body in a confined space, are they?' Freed from the impediment of skates, I hardly believed it myself.

Leticia doodled in her notebook. 'Don't worry about that. I'll convince them it was all perfectly natural. Now, I just need you to detail the last events at the party to give me the full picture. Did anything else happen?'

The party got going when Donny and Tracy turned up the music and pushed back the tables. Filled with sugar and alcohol, the guests had no hesitation in letting rip to 'Great Balls of Fire'. Donny had fantastic rhythm, and he twirled Tracy around as if she were weightless. Her face shone with undiluted joy, and despite her carping attitude, their obvious love for each other gave me a warm glow.

Ryan prowled at the edge of the action. At one point, he grabbed Jade's waist and pulled her towards him. Struggling to balance her tray of drinks, she protested, but he wouldn't let go. I was just about to rush out from behind the counter when Gloria pinballed into the back of his legs.

She made a show of apologising, but Ryan pushed her away, jerked back his shoulders and strutted towards my counter, where Graham had left a moment before. Tia-Marie stood alone like a damsel tied to a post.

Scanning the crowd, I located his grey head bent over Pauline. She was clutching his jacket lapels.

'I'll get a Jack D and Coke,' said Ryan. 'And whatever Tia-Marie wants.'

She stared ahead. 'I'm fine.'

'C'mon, hun, don't be boring. Loosen up.' Sticking out his tongue, he lifted the lower part of his top, revealing tattooed arrows pointing below.

I shared a pained glance with Tia-Marie.

'Graham's coming back,' I lied, thinking it might dislodge the pest.

'So what?' Ryan gyrated his hips at Tia-Marie. 'Think what I could do for you, hun.'

Give me dandruff any day. 'Yep, he's just on his way.'

That was perhaps stretching the truth. As I peered across the room, Pauline slapped Graham and ran out of the room. He stood for a moment before rushing after her.

As Ryan piled on the sleaze, I kept my eyes on the door, willing it to open and for Graham to return. But I should have realised Tia-Marie could take care of herself.

Slipping down from the stool, she towered over Ryan. 'C'mon then, *hun.* Let's see what you're made of.' Thrusting her golden globes forward, she pushed him towards the dance area. Ryan lost his swagger and faltered.

Nobody appeared to notice them at first. The dancers had gathered around Donny and Tracy, who were putting on an energetic show to 'Rockin' Robin'.

Tia-Marie clasped Ryan's head to her magnificent breasts, then circled her arms around him. His body sagged as she swayed them around the floor.

'Watch out for the fireworks,' said Gloria, parking herself at my counter. 'God, will this night never end? I've had enough.'

'Me too.' Jade pulled up beside her. 'My poor feet. Oh no, look! What's happening now?'

The jukebox's lights blinked a distress call before juddering to a halt. The crowd groaned and then parted as Donny ran towards the ailing machine. Sweat ran down his face. Perhaps it had run into his eyes. He missed the jukebox, cannonballed into the swaying entity of Ryan and Tia-Marie, and knocked them down like Skittles.

Tracy dived into the tangled heap. 'Get off my fiancé, you tart.'

I buried my face in the tea towel, but Gloria snatched it away. 'You can't miss this.'

Tia-Marie extracted herself first. Rising like Venus, she stepped to one side and smoothed down her dress. But she'd underestimated her opponent. Tracy yanked at the strappy high heels.

'Tia's gone totally arse over whatsit.' Gloria gasped. 'Tracy's like a woman possessed.'

'Savage,' agreed Jade.

Revelling in the carnage, the guests had turned into Roman spectators, baying for blood. Donny flailed from side to side like a grounded, fat sheep. The two women, shrieking like fishwives, slapped each other across his expanse. Like a coward, Ryan tried to crawl away, but Graham, who'd appeared from nowhere, stamped on his hands.

I clutched at Gloria. 'We need to do something. This could get serious.'

'Like what? Who'd want to charge into the middle of that?' She pulled a face. 'On roller skates!'

Graham struggled to pull Tracy and Tia-Marie apart but fell flat on his face between them.

Ryan's next action shocked me. After dragging himself up by the legs of a table, he seized two bottles, smashed them together, and headed back towards Graham.

I screamed. 'Stop him.'

The crowd came to their senses, and two burly men grabbed Ryan and dragged him outside.

The jukebox kicked back into life and treated us to 'What a Wonderful World'.

Leticia put down her pen. 'Sounds like a riot. Our murder victim had an eventful last night.'

'He certainly did.' I sat up straighter. 'And none of it involved me. There should be plenty for the police to go on.'

'Indeed. And did the party end there?'

'More or less. Donny still insisted on cutting the cake and making a speech. Can you believe it? Tracy dusted herself down, and Pauline reappeared. I'd hardly seen her all night. She seemed detached, as if she didn't care any more.'

Leticia leaned back and stretched. 'What about the others?'

'I didn't see Ryan again. Graham put Tia-Marie into a taxi and then came back inside. After the guests had gone, Pauline told us to leave, as the family had things to discuss.'

Closing her notebook, Leticia smiled. 'I bet they did. Now, Helen, are you ready for your police interview?'

Two grim-faced men confronted me across a scruffy desk in a bare, grey room. The strip light cast an unflattering glow, making even Leticia's English rose complexion seem sallow. Sitting beside me, she squeezed my arm.

They'd done all the official bits: the caution, the introductions, and the fiddling about with the recording equipment. Too nervous to concentrate, I'd already forgotten their names.

The senior one, Inspector something, had panther-sleek hair and one of those complexions that never looked clean. The exact expression describing such a face floated beyond my grasp.

Frowning, I turned my gaze to his colleague, Constable, whatever he'd said. Floppy-haired and boyish, he'd possibly not started shaving yet.

The inspector raised his voice and rapped on the desk. 'Ms Merang, are you listening?' His opaque eyes narrowed, and his chin seemed to have grown even darker. With such satanic features, he could well have been up all night hunting for blood.

He had a permanent five o'clock shadow; that was it. Pleased that my memory was still functioning, I gave a self-congratulatory nod.

The officers exchanged a look, which plainly said, 'We've got a right one here'.

Inspector Dracula sighed. 'I was asking how well you knew the victim, Mr Graham Sutty?'

'A little.'

'Can you expand on that?'

'He had terrible dandruff.'

The constable snorted and received a glare from his boss.

'Anything else?'

'He fell out with all the Donoghues last night. Have you asked them?'

Dracula glared. 'I'm asking you, Ms Merang. *You* were the one caught with blood on your hands.'

'Blood on your hands,' echoed the constable.

'I thought it was jam.'

Leticia leaned forward. 'Is this relevant, Inspector? You've already found the blood had been spilt hours before my client arrived on the scene.'

Scowling, the inspector clasped his hands together. 'Your client has keys to the premises and could have accessed them day or night.'

I fixed my gaze on the inspector's hands. Hands that a werewolf would not be ashamed to call his own. I wondered if his legs were just as hairy.

Leticia gave a well-bred snort. 'My client is not even two weeks into her job at Donny's Diner. She had no previous knowledge of the victim. A man, I might add, who was known to all the Donoghues in both a personal and professional capacity.' Ignoring the growl in the inspector's throat, she ploughed on. 'During an eventful last night, Mr Sutty argued with three members of the family and was the victim of two separate acts of violence in front of witnesses. One by Mrs Donoghue, and also one by her stepdaughter's fiancé, who needed restraining. My client was first on the scene this morning as she had cleaning duties to perform, as outlined in her job description.'

Leticia sat back in her chair. I could have kissed her. It was like having Boadicea batting for your team. Why had James let such a gem slip through his fingers?

'Putting all that to one side,' said the inspector, turning his gimlet eyes back to me. 'The fact remains, Ms Merang, you were discovered trying to wash vital evidence down the sink.'

'One of my jobs is to clean the kitchen.' Leticia had given me confidence, and I pulled my back straight. 'My attention was immediately drawn to the dirty knife.'

The inspector raised his dark brow. 'I commend your attention to detail, but that leaves me perplexed. Yes, I'm very perplexed.'

His junior also declared himself perplexed.

I gritted my teeth. 'By what?'

'The kitchen is quite small, I believe?' The inspector circled his arm. 'No bigger than this room, in fact?'

I nodded. 'About the same.'

The inspector drew back his top lip, revealing two jagged canine teeth. 'Ms Merang, we've established your attention to detail is second to none. Upon entering a confined space, you immediately saw a ten-inch knife, but seemingly failed to notice a dead man – all six feet of him – lying nearby.'

'I ... I ...' How to convince him my ineptitude on roller skates had affected my focus? It didn't even seem plausible to me.

'Yes, Ms Merang?' He tipped back on his chair with a nasty sneer on his lips. 'Take all the time you need, on top of the many hours you've already had to concoct an explanation.'

My legs started shaking, and fog clouded my brain. 'Well, the thing is ... I mean, have you ever tried roller sk—' A sharp tap on my knee stopped me. 'No comment.'

We all folded our arms and stared across the table at each other. A loud knock on the door broke the impasse, and a man stuck his head into the room.

'Inspector, can I have a word?' Jiggling his eyebrows, he added, 'It's urgent.'

With a deep sigh, the inspector rose and announced his departure to the recording system. 'Please excuse me, ladies. I won't be long.' He planted a heavy hand on the constable's shoulder as if pressing him into the ground.

The mood lightened as soon as he left. None of us spoke. I concentrated on breathing slowly and deeply. My heart was banging away like a military band.

After a couple of minutes, Leticia rapped on the table. 'Constable, did you not hear the inspector?'

I looked towards the door in surprise. I'd not heard anything.

The constable dropped the goofy expression. 'Sorry, what did you say?'

'The inspector has been calling you. Sounds like he's getting impatient.'

In his haste to rise, the man pushed the desk so hard it rammed into our stomachs. 'Sorry, sorry.' He headed for the door, but Leticia called him back.

'Constable, for the benefit of the tape, you have to—'

'I know. I was just about to do it.' He cleared his throat and announced he was leaving the room.

As the door slammed behind him, Leticia put a finger to her lips and rose from her chair.

I nodded but had to choke down an exclamation at what she did next. Seconds later, a kerfuffle sounded outside the door.

'You stupid idiot, Harper. Don't give me that.'

Someone yanked open the door. The inspector stepped in, glared at me, but then lifted his heavy brows as if something were amiss. 'Where's she gone?'

I couldn't trust myself to speak.

'The chair beside you is empty.' The inspector spelt out his words as if I'd gone deaf. 'Where is your solicitor?'

'I'm over here.'

'What the—' He spun towards the voice.

'I'm lying here dead, Inspector. All five-feet-ten of me sprawled out on the floor.'

Standing at the police station exit, I gulped my first taste of freedom. In my tatty, cheap nylon frills, I might have looked like a clapped-out cheerleader who'd lost her squad, but I wanted to punch the air in triumph. I'd told the police to donate my skates to charity.

Leticia placed an arm around my shoulders. 'C'mon, you must be freezing in that flimsy outfit. I'll give you a lift home.'

Installed in her plush, comfy Audi, I sighed in relief. 'I never want to go back there. I won't have to, will I?' My toes curled up at the prospect.

'Hopefully not. You're not on police bail. They've released you under investigation. It should have been without charge. That inspector was just being awkward.' Starting up the car, she frowned. 'Maybe I shouldn't have played that silly trick.'

'It was worth it though, wasn't it? His face! So, do they still think I'm involved?'

Negotiating a tricky roundabout, she took a while to answer. 'Possibly, but it means they have little or no evidence to charge you. It's pretty standard practice, but unfortunately, it means you're in limbo.'

'But for how long?' Panic rose in my stomach.

Leticia took her eyes off the road to crack a sympathetic smile. 'That's the tricky bit, I'm afraid. It's indefinite – or at least until the case is solved.'

Despite the warmth of the car, my shivering increased. 'So if it's never solved, I'll always be under suspicion for murder?'

'I'm afraid so. But try not to worry. Let's keep positive.'

Bye Bye Bedsit

Leticia gasped when we entered my litter-infested street. As I directed her to my building, I cringed at the sheets pinned up at the downstairs windows, the graffiti on the wall, and the kicked-in front door.

'Crikey,' she said under her breath.

I tried to make light. 'It's a palace inside.'

'I got the impression life wasn't too rosy for you at the moment, but I never expected this. Oh, Helen, what—'

'It's only temporary. In fact, more temporary than I planned.' Seeing it through Leticia's eyes had made me reconsider. 'Sorry to impose on you further, but could you possibly take me to a hotel once I've grabbed some clothes?'

She smiled. 'No problem. I'll wait here. I've got a few calls to make.'

I ran up the narrow stairs to my garret as fast as my slapping slippers would allow.

Leticia drove me to one of the city centre's budget-chain hotels. After my bedsit, it would be a luxurious haven. It could go on my credit card until the money came through from our property sales. I'd wanted to save money by taking the crummy bedsit, but I didn't care any more.

She pulled up at a nondescript doorway on a street full of bars and restaurants. Incarceration must have warped my sense of time. At the police station, I'd gauged Saturday night to be in full swing, but it was only just starting.

Groups of shrieking girls, arm in arm, surged through the street in confident waves. Packs of men parted in their wake before turning to assess the rear view. In the first flush of alcohol, the air fizzed with high expectations. I would request a room at the back. In my fragile state, I couldn't face the carnage that would inevitably round off the night.

Leticia handed me her business card. 'Keep in touch.'

'Of course, and you'll need to send me your bill.'

'Don't worry about that. James said he'd take care of it. After all, what are friends for?'

Twenty minutes later in my small, clean room, with the softest bed ever, I mulled over Leticia's remark. Ever since James poured wet clay over my head at primary school, and I shoved glue down his shorts, we'd been best friends forever.

James! He must be worried sick. Anxious to put his mind at rest, I grabbed my phone.

He took ages to answer. 'Hey, jailbird. I take it you've escaped?'

'Leticia was brilliant. Thanks so much. I'm so grateful, I want—'

'Sorry, Hels, I'm just on my way to—'

'God, it's been the second-worst day of my life. I might even upgrade it to the—'

'I bet, but can we talk tomorrow?'

'What? You're not going out, are you?' My voice rose to a screech. 'How could you, while I'm in a police cell, facing a murder charge, cast off from society, subject to police brutality, corruption and lies?'

He laughed. 'But you're not. Where *are* you, by the way?'

'A Mint hotel. But that's not the point. You should have still been fretting about me.'

'What if I said I was only going out as a distraction?'

I forced hurt into my voice. 'You should have been sick with worry. What sort of friend are you?'

'Hels, it's Saturday night. I'm a young, single, red-blooded male. It's my duty to be out there.'

I sighed. 'Weren't you even a tiny bit anxious?'

'A bucket-full, but I knew Leticia would spring you. Look, I've got to go, but we'll speak tomorrow, yeah? Why don't you ring Prue?'

'Okay, bye.' He'd already gone. 'Wish you were here,' I whispered to the silent room.

But James was right. I should ring Prue. I scrolled down my contacts to the ancient photo by her name. Beaming at the camera, she was standing on a pebbly beach, arm in arm with my mum. They must only have been teenagers. Prue's beehive was still in its infancy. If not for the evidence of that photo, I'd have thought she'd been born a stern, middle-aged matron. Such a bittersweet memory. I wished my mum's face was more in focus.

Dear old Prue. Despite her insular ways, she'd tucked me under her prickly wing when I needed her the most, and it would be a comfort to hear her voice.

My finger hovered over the call button. But I couldn't mention my ordeal. Not without giving her a cardiac arrest.

That struck a chord. On a Saturday night, she'd be glued to *Casualty* and probably wouldn't even answer her phone.

Switching on the telly, I tuned into *Casualty,* with the silly notion I was sharing it with Prue. At least it would do as background noise. I resolved to ring her the next day.

I unpacked the holdall and hung my meagre threads in the wardrobe. Conscious of keeping Leticia waiting in my dismal street, I'd been too hasty with my selection of clothes. Nothing matched.

Stripping off my uniform, I hurled it triumphantly into the bin. After a second's thought, I retrieved it. No doubt Tracy would charge me if I didn't hand it back. She'd be slapping on a fine for the roller skates as it was.

In the pristine bathroom, the shower ran hot and powerful. I stayed there for ages, inhaling the milk and honey perfume of the hotel's toiletries – worth every penny of the extra two pounds per night.

In dazed contentment, I reached for an amazingly soft towel, all cosy and warm from the heated rail. Zack and I had enjoyed weekends away in luxurious spa hotels in exotic locations, but I'd never appreciated them as much as that budget one in Leeds.

Wrapped up snug in the hotel dressing gown – an extra one pound fifty a night – I sat on the bed and rang Gloria. No answer. I tried Jade. She didn't pick up. But what did I expect? It was Saturday night, and they had their own lives to lead.

From the holdall, I pulled out my globe and placed it on the bedside table. No way would I have left behind my last link to Zack. I gave it a spin, wondering where he might be. 'Hey,

Zack, I was arrested for murder today. Thought you might want to know.'

I considered climbing into bed, burrowing under the covers, and putting the nightmare of a day behind me. But I was too wired to sleep.

I could have ordered room service but had no appetite. I would make a hot chocolate from one of the sachets and watch the telly. The kettle had just boiled when my phone rang. Gloria's name flashed on the display, and I nearly scalded my arm in my rush to get to it.

'Hi, Helen. Sorry, got to be quick. Are you okay? I've been sick with worry all day.'

'Where are you? You sound like you're whispering in a box.'

'In the downstairs loo at my in-laws. Mobiles are banned. They say I've got to set an example to the boys. Jeez, it does my head in. Please tell me you're all right. Tracy said the police took you away in handcuffs.'

'They had to let me go. Not enough evidence ... but ... oh, I'll tell you later. What happened at the diner?'

'Sorry, Mabel's calling me. I've got to go. Just wanted to check on you. I can breathe again now. Listen, let's meet up tomorrow. I'll arrange it with Jade. She's been in tears about you all day. Ring you in the morning.'

'Bye.' I gulped, and my eyes welled up. The phone fell from my hand, and I suddenly felt weary.

The sun shone through the thin curtains. In my bedsit, I'd trained myself not to stretch. My banana crate couldn't take it, and I'd end up banging my feet on the sink. That morning, on my comfy, proper-sized mattress, I extended my legs and stretched out for England.

I reached for my phone and gasped. Five minutes past ten. How had I slept so long? And what had I missed? My screen displayed a gratifying number of missed calls and messages.

Four voicemails from James. His first one wished me a good night's sleep. In the next, his drunken mates sang an unsavoury lullaby. By the third, the "bastards" had left him, and all the women were minging. Finally, he'd lost the keys to his apartment. I was his only true friend, and he wanted to see me right this minute.

He'd kill me if I woke him up now. I winced at my word choice. With poor Graham dead on the slab, I should be more mindful.

Gloria had sent a couple of messages – the last one read, **Meet you at Bill's for brunch at eleven?**

I bounded out of bed and into the bathroom.

Rushing into Bill's an hour later, I found my friends sitting in a corner under a bicycle wheel chandelier. I squeezed onto the hard bench beside them and placed my bag on the upturned boat of a table.

Jade grasped my hand. 'Were the police truly horrible? Did they lock you up in a filthy cell with violent scumbag criminals?'

Before I could reply, Gloria butted in. 'You watch too much telly. But go on, Helen, we're dying to know.'

While we stuffed ourselves with bacon, eggs, and hash browns, I related all that had happened. 'The thing is,' I said as we finally pushed away our grease-smeared plates, 'I'm still under suspicion, and it's really bugging me. It's hard to move forward with that hanging over my head.'

'Like a noose,' said Jade. 'I see what you mean. Everyone'll still think you did it.'

Gloria frowned. 'Jade, that's not helpful.'

My stomach dropped. 'But she's right.'

'No,' said Gloria in a firm voice. 'The police are bound to find the real murderer, and then you'll be off the hook.'

'What if they don't, though?' persisted Jade. 'My dad said they were useless when his car got nicked.'

'Jade!' Gloria shouted so loud, the people at the next table stopped eating.

'Now you know my side,' I said, 'tell me what happened at the diner.'

Jade leaned forward in excitement. 'The police interviewed us and took our fingerprints. Can you believe it?'

'Start at the beginning,' said Gloria.

'Oh, okay. Well, we arrived at the diner together, didn't we, Gloria? And it was all cordoned off by police tape – and we had to say who we were, 'cause they weren't going to let us in at first. It was really exciting. Obvs we didn't know there'd been a murder – that Graham was lying there, dead – but we knew something serious had happened all right, didn't we, Glo?'

Gloria raised her eyes to meet mine. 'Obvs. I did wonder if Donny had blown himself up in a cooking-related incident.'

'The police told us to sit in the corner away from the kitchen,' continued Jade. 'We still didn't know what had happened, but Tracy was there, crying. Then Donny and Pauline arrived and sat apart from each other, stone-faced. Pauline looked even more miserable than usual, so they must have already known. She put her arms around Tracy, but that seemed to make her even more upset. When Tracy pulled herself together a bit, she said she'd found you with the knife. I couldn't believe it.' She patted my hand. 'I didn't believe you'd done it, not for a second.'

'Of course not,' said Gloria. 'But someone killed Graham. And I can't see it being a random stranger. There were a lot of bad vibes at that party.'

My heart raced as I mulled over her words. 'Do you mean … it was—?'

'A Donoghue?' said Gloria. 'Yes, I do. Or someone close to them at least.'

Jade spluttered out her drink. 'You can't mean that, Glo. I know they're a bit mad, but even so? I don't think my mum would like me working for murderers. But I need the money, and it took me ages to find a job.'

'Me too,' said Gloria. 'It's scary when you've been out of the job market so long.'

I tightened the grip on my fork. 'Well, I definitely won't be going back.'

'Tracy said she wouldn't have you at any price,' said Jade. 'She was a bit nasty about it, actually.'

Gloria glared at Jade. 'What's got into you today? You're about as subtle as a knife in the back.'

Jade clapped a hand over her mouth.

'It's fine. Tracy never liked me.' I grinned at Jade to show no hard feelings. 'Donny's invested a lot of money in the diner, but will he feel like reopening?'

They both nodded, and Jade looked at Gloria. 'Definitely. We overheard him saying to Tracy, "This could be good for business. It'll get the rubber-necking punters flocking in".'

I shrugged. 'That doesn't surprise me. Murder as a marketing ploy. I suppose it's as good a motive as any to kill Graham. I can't think of any other. Who'd want to kill him? He seemed such a boring, nondescript bloke.'

'On the face of it,' agreed Gloria. 'But why did he bring Tia-Marie to the party? That seemed like a deliberate act of provocation.'

She had a point. 'I suppose it did cause a stir.'

Gloria slammed down her cup. 'I'm convinced. Tia-Marie's at the heart of it all, and he was killed because of her. The thing is, what are we going to do about it?'

My mind went blank, and Jade held out her hands in a hopeless gesture.

Gloria repeated her challenge and added, 'There's a killer out there.'

'Keep your voice down,' I said, as heads turned, and a child started to bawl.

'Okay, but I'm serious. We need to be proactive.' Gloria's eyes flashed like crazy disco lights. 'I'd have thought you'd be right up for it, Helen, seeing as it affects you the most. But actually, it casts a shadow over us all.'

'The police will have it in hand,' I persisted. 'They know what they're doing.'

Gloria snorted. 'What, by arresting you? Maybe Inspector Dracula's capable, but Constable Harper's what my mother would call a "clot".'

'Oh, I thought he was cute,' said Jade. 'He was very friendly when he took my statement.'

I held up my palm. 'But Gloria, you said the police would soon find the real murderer.'

She shrugged. 'Just trying to make you feel better.'

My mouth had turned dry. 'Poking our noses into this could be dangerous. And besides, where would we even start?'

'We'd be discreet. Just ask a few questions to the right people, starting with Tia-Marie.'

'But how would we contact her?' asked Jade.

'Ryan seemed to know Tia-Marie from school, but who'd want to tackle him?' I folded my arms. 'No, Gloria. It's too risky to get involved. If it's Donoghue-related, we're far too close. Especially with you and Jade still working there.'

Gloria stuck out her chin. 'But if you'd heard what I—'

'Helen's right, Glo.' Jade's face had turned pale. My mum would kill me if I ... well, you know what I mean.'

'What a bloody pair of yellow-bellies.' Gloria sighed. 'Okay, you win. We'll leave it to Dracula and his clot.' The glint in her eye said otherwise.

Parting from my friends, I decided a brisk walk to Ampsley would do me good after being cooped up in that police cell. Besides, I needed to collect more clothes.

My scruffy street seemed busy for a Sunday afternoon. As I hurried along, a nervous flutter rose in my stomach. Though not cold, I zipped up my jacket and pulled down the hood.

I stopped before reaching my shared house. A crowd had gathered outside. I approached a woman standing on the edge. 'What's going on?'

'It's the press, love, innit? A murderer lives there.'

Bloody Hell. 'Is the murderer in there now?'

'Dunno. Think they've done a bunk, but it's great, innit? They're gonna start filming in a minute.' The woman pushed greasy strands out of her eyes. 'See that van over there? Guess who's in it.'

Lassie? Kylie Minogue? 'I've no idea. Who?'

'Only that Lindy Peeps.'

'Really?' I must have looked blank.

'You know? From that new media channel, *Let's Look at Leeds.*' The woman nudged me. 'Look! She's getting out of the van.'

The press parted, and a woman in shiny black boots marched up my path. Her cute pink fur coat flapped open, revealing a tight, lacy dress.

'She always looks lovely,' said my companion. 'And she speaks very nice.'

Lindy posed in front of the kicked-in door while the camera crew got their act together. Her strident voice rang out in the street. 'This once affluent neighbourhood has descended into a web of drugs, vice and ...' She grasped for another crime. 'And the like.'

A bit weak, Lindy. Lassie might have done better.

'Within these very walls, I imagine a deviant mind might have planned their bloodthirsty crime.' Lindy paused and flung out her arm. 'It wouldn't surprise me if, beyond this disgusting door of a possible drug den beats the merciless heart of an alleged killer.' She lowered her voice and looked directly into the camera. 'This heartless murderer – alleged – remains the focus of a major police investigation.'

My "merciless" heart pounded in my ears. And apart from anything else, I wanted to challenge Lindy's inconsistent narrative on hearts, alleged or otherwise.

Rounding it off with a shiver and a brave smile, she drew the fluffy coat around her. 'Lindy Peeps, bringing the streets of Leeds into your home.'

'Better than *EastEnders,* innit?' said the woman. 'I only nipped out for some milk. Get yourself home, lass. These streets aren't safe with a murderer on the loose.'

'I will, thanks. Bye.'

I was a fugitive. I'd never felt so isolated and alone. Paranoia took hold, and I scuttled away before anyone recognised me. If the police didn't come up with the real murderer soon, this could be just the start. Even Zack – in the arse end of wherever he was – might hear about it. At least Lindy hadn't named me. But someone had supplied my address, so surely the press knew my name?

Buttersley Two-Five-Two-Four

I ran most of the three miles back to the city centre, but nearing my hotel, I forced myself to walk. I'd half expected Lindy Peeps to be outside doing her "heartless" stuff, but the coast was clear. Pulling down my hood, I fluffed up my curls and sauntered through the door, as if my life was as sweet as cherry pie.

The woman in reception didn't even raise her head as I headed towards the lift. Any other time, I might have found it annoying, but her indifference suited me nicely. In my room, I let out a huge sigh of relief. After drawing the curtains against the dismal day and flicking on the lamps, my mood lifted, and I stretched out on the bed.

I must have dozed off, as my ringing phone made me start. My drunken friend had resurfaced. 'Hi, James. How's the hangover?'

'One of the worst.' He groaned. 'Why do I do it? How's freedom? Have you recovered from your ordeal?'

'I've been Lindy Peeped.'

'What?'

I filled him in.

'Run that by me again. You've been living in a bedsit in Ampsley? I don't believe you.'

'Shut up. That's not the point. What if the press starts hounding me? What am I going to do then?'

'Come back to London and stay with me.'

'No way. You've got glass doors on your bathrooms and white leather sofas.'

'Though a stranger to good taste, you must know it makes sense to get out of Leeds.'

'I'm not running away.' I raised my voice. 'I've done nothing wrong.'

'Okay. The offer's there if you need it.'

'Thanks, James. I really appreciate it. And did I thank you properly for Leticia and for paying her bill?'

'It's your birthday and Christmas presents for the next ten years.'

'Will you be updating Zack?' James always denied they were in contact, but I had my suspicions. They'd been mates long before James introduced us, and after all, Zack left *me*, not James.

'No, but you should perhaps alert Prue. If the press knows your identity ...'

I clutched my throat. 'They could trace me back to Buttersley and turn up on Prue's doorstep.'

James laughed. 'God help 'em if they do.'

I quickly said goodbye to James and steeled myself to ring Prue. What time was it? Just gone four. She was probably having a nap after Sunday lunch. I wouldn't want to wake her, but what if the pack was on its way? What if the reporters were already there?

As always, Prue's phone rang and rang. The relic resided in the chilly hinterland of her hallway, sitting on its own little table by the hard, faux-leather banquette. She'd probably be in her lounge, reaching down to turn the electric fire off first. When I lived there after Mum died, she was forever telling me, "It's criminal to waste heat on an empty room".

My mind wandered to her other sayings, so I jumped when her irritated voice sounded in my ear.

'Buttersley two-five-two-four. I repeat, Buttersley two-five-two-four. Who is on the line, please?'

'It's me! Sorry, I was miles away. And you've got to add a lot more digits in now.'

'I like my number as it is, thank you very much. So, have you rung to lecture me on the mysterious ways of British Telecom?'

'Hello, Prue. How are you?'

'I'm very well, my girl. I was just thinking it's about time I heard from you, but I suppose you're so busy with your hectic life in London.'

'I'm not in London any more. I couldn't stay there after Zack went. I'm in Leeds now and coming to see you soon.'

'Are you indeed? Not before time.' She failed to hide the pleasure in her voice.

'The thing is ...' Where the hell should I start? I plunged in with an edited version of my current situation and ended with, 'I'm concerned about you. What if the press turns up on your doorstep?'

'Highly unlikely. They wouldn't have the wit to trace you back here. But in any case, don't you worry about me. I shall keep my broom by the door. And I'll alert Mr Wilberforce. He'll set his hosepipe on them.' She sniffed. 'He needs no excuse to use it.'

'He's still next door, is he? He must be eighty by now.'

'Eighty-four. Still the old soldier. So, let's get this straight, you've been working in Leeds – not twenty miles away – and you didn't see fit to tell me?'

I thought I'd got away with that one, assuming she'd be more preoccupied with the murder. 'It was only ever going to be temporary, Prue. I was just getting some work experience.'

'Experience in frying doughnuts? You've been to university. You've got a degree and all those fancy certificates in ... whatever. All that studying.' She tutted. 'For what?'

'To do something I've been wanting to do for a long time.' I took a deep breath and crossed my fingers. 'I want to open my own confectionery shop and tea room.'

'In Leeds? It's never been the same since they closed Schofields and Lewis's.'

I paused. 'No, in Buttersley. I want to come home.'

'Oh.'

When she didn't follow that up, I looked at my screen to see if we were still connected. 'Are you there?'

'Yes.' She coughed. 'Just a little tickle. Excuse me. I need to blow my nose.' When she returned, she had a catch in her voice. 'I was just going to say it was your mum's dream. Well, both our dreams, really. We were always going to open a little tea shop together on the high street.'

'Were you? You've never told me that before. So, you approve?'

'Of course. I will support you in any way I can.'

Time for a lump to enter my throat. 'Thanks, Prue. That means such a lot.'

'Just a few things for you to clear up first, my girl. I have every faith in the police. You just need to keep your head down while they find the real culprit. But then, you never listen to me. Take care of yourself.'

Prue's backing had reignited my spark. With her behind me, I could achieve anything. I'd start looking for suitable premises immediately.

I'd just put the phone down when Gloria rang. She sounded breathless.

'Helen, I'm so sorry.'

'For what?'

'For going on like I did at Bill's. Banging on about suspects and that. Think I scared poor Jade. That's why I shut up. But the thing is, the reason I got so worked up, I overheard an argument at the party. I think it might be relevant to the murder.'

A Praying Mantis

I gripped my phone. 'What argument? Who was it between?'

Gloria dodged my questions. 'It was before the fight broke out. I needed to get away from the customers, so I headed for that dark alcove in the corridor to take a quick break. I was just minding my own business behind the coat stand when a door slammed and feet marched towards me.'

'Who was it?'

'I froze and hoped they wouldn't come any nearer. They stopped only feet away, and I stood there like a lemon, holding my breath. Thought my uniform would pop, and I'd burst out all over them.'

I clicked my teeth with impatience. 'And who would you be bursting out all over?'

'Wait a minute. I'm getting to that. Thought it was Tracy, come looking for me, but it didn't sound like her trotters. It seemed to be two people, but I didn't have a clue until they started whispering. Seemed like they were arguing.' She paused. 'Have you ever tried it? Arguing in whispers, I mean. It hurts your jaw.'

'Never mind about jaws. Who was it?'

She laughed. 'Haven't you sussed it yet? Graham and Pauline, of course.'

'Right. That must have been after she slapped him. She stormed off, and he followed.'

'If you say so. I was lurking in the shadows, remember?'

'Like a praying mantis.'

'What are you on about? Do you want to hear this or what?'

I caught her excitement. 'Of course. Carry on.'

Gloria took a deep preparatory breath. 'Graham acted all hurt at first. "Why did you do that, Pauline? You've shown us both up." All that sort of guff. At the time, I didn't know Pauline had slapped him. She hissed he'd brought a tart to the party. He didn't seem put out by that. In fact, he got a bit cocky – well, as much as a boring bloke with dandruff can be. "Jealous, are you?" he said in a sort of sly, mocking way.'

I sat on the bed. 'Sounds like he was goading her.'

'Definitely. Pauline didn't answer, but this is where it got interesting. Graham said, "You were cruel to me. You'd always had a thing for Donny, and after Liz, you saw your chance. You said he was dynamic, and I irritated you. Called me predictable. Well, I'm not predictable tonight, am I?" Can you believe it?'

I clicked through my memory. 'Mmm, we knew they had history together, didn't we?'

'Did we?'

I pictured Gloria creasing her freckled brow. 'When Pauline brought Graham to our training session, Donny accused them both of being boring and said they should have stayed together. Don't you remember?'

'Vaguely. Anyway, then Pauline changed her tune. Said his tactic of bringing the tart had worked, and she *was* jealous. Then she went all girlie.'

'What do you mean?'

'This is Pauline.' Gloria assumed a falsetto. '"Graham, I've been such a fool. I was dazzled and taken in by Donny, but now I see him for what he is. I just want you". That's exactly what she said.'

'And what did he say to that performance?'

My friend deepened her tone. '"Too late. You and Donny deserve each other. You jumped into his bed when Liz's side was still warm. And now it's not working out with that fat windbag, you think you can crawl back to me". God, I can't keep this up.' Gloria broke into a coughing fit.

'Love the acting. You're wasted at Donny's.'

'I know. Graham then stuck the metaphorical knife in. Said it was delightful to have such an attractive girl on his arm, as opposed to a dowdy frump like Pauline.'

'Ouch. Bet she could have killed him for that,' I said without thinking.

'Pauline understandably got nasty back. Reminded him he was paying for it, and that a young woman like Tia-Marie wouldn't be seen dead with him otherwise. Graham said at least he could afford it, not like her wastrel husband. He finished with, "Will you even make the latest loan repayment?"' Gloria sighed. 'Got to go now. The boys need feeding. They're prowling like wolves.'

'Just before you go, don't you think we should tell the police about this? It sounds important.'

'I did. Inspector Dracula didn't seem too interested but said they'd look into it. I got the impression he thought I'd made it all up. The cheek. Gotta go now. Speak tomorrow.'

I placed the phone on the bed and sat for a while, going over our conversation. Maybe I should tell Leticia about this? Who would have thought Pauline had passionate depths? So the argument explained why Gloria had been so adamant that Tia-Marie was at the crux of it all. But I couldn't help thinking she'd got the wrong end of the hot dog. Tia-Marie might be pivotal, but not for that reason. I recalled the argument *I'd* overheard between Graham and Donny. Graham claimed Tia-Marie had confirmed his worst suspicions about Donny. But I didn't have a clue what they were.

I'd stayed still for so long, my legs had cramped. Stretching out, I yawned. Still tired from my ordeal the previous day, I would watch a bit of telly and have an early night. I ordered a selection of newspapers for the morning and switched on an episode of *Midsomer Murders*.

A sharp knock on the hotel door awoke me. I'd been fast asleep, dreaming of doughnuts. I bolted upright with my heart pounding. The room was still in darkness. Who could it be? The police? The press? Don't say they'd managed to track me down. No further knocks, but they wouldn't just go away like that, would they? I clapped a hand to my head. Stupid girl. It was Monday morning, and my newspapers had arrived. That was all.

I stumbled out of bed, tripped over my discarded shoes, and limped to the door. After scanning the empty corridor, I scooped up my papers, turned on the light and braced myself. Even so, I still shrieked at the headline of the *Morning Post*.

The Cutest Cat in Town

My hands shook as I scanned the headline of the local paper. 'The Hunt is on For Helen Merang'. The byline said the prime suspect in the doughnut murder had abandoned her Ampsley lair and disappeared into thin air.

'Have you seen this woman?' By the side of a horrendously bad copy of my passport photo, they advised their readers not to approach me.

Blank eyes stared out from beneath a concrete fringe. My nose had all but disappeared, and a solid black line replaced my lips. I'd run a mile if I came up against such a troll.

How dare they release my photo? I didn't look human, but that wasn't the point. Where was data protection when you needed it? It could only have come from Donny's. In my job application, they'd needed to verify my identity, and I'd watched Pauline photocopy my passport and churn out that monster. It probably wasn't a priority for the Donoghues, but they needed to get that copier fixed. They must also have provided my Ampsley address. It surely wouldn't have come from the police.

Hopefully, no one would recognise me from such a poor likeness. The *Morning Post* had also added another twelve years to my age. Any other time, I'd be fuming, but it could work in my favour. But I still wouldn't be rushing out anytime soon.

Donny's Diner had issued a statement at what they termed 'this difficult time for us'. They could hardly believe I was a murderer, but I *was* a misfit who'd not slotted into their family team. And it came as no surprise to them that I'd stolen an expensive pair of roller skates. My cheeks burned with rage.

The rest of the statement raved on about the diner and how Donny resolved to carry on in the face of such tragedy. Apparently, it's what the family's accountant would have wanted. Mr Graham Sutty had been such an enthusiastic supporter of their exciting new venture.

So, my full name was out there. I'd been right to warn Prue. She had taken the *Morning Post* ever since I was a teenager and had always enjoyed a rant over the editor's long-standing feud with the council.

If I dared leave my room, I'd have to be careful walking through the hotel. I burrowed my face in my hands. Oh no, the receptionist had taken an imprint of my credit card. They'd soon realise that the prime suspect, Helen Merang, was a guest. Perhaps running back to London was the best option after all?

James needed to know I was on my way. Where the hell was my phone? I shook the duvet, and as the phone dropped on the floor, my credit card slipped out of the cover. Reaching down, the name on the card caught my attention: Miss H Chandler.

'That's me,' I announced to the silent room. Changing it to my married name of Merang had been on my to-do list for the last seven years. I could have cried in relief.

Still holding the phone, I jumped when it rang.

'Am I speaking to the fugitive from justice?' Gloria gave one of her snorts.

I held the phone away. 'Gloria, you need to know that's not an attractive sound.'

'Who'd have thought you were so photogenic?'

'Shut up or I'll pinch your roller skates.'

Gloria laughed, but not for long. 'Seriously, this is an outrage. I really feel for you. I bet Tracy gave 'em that photo and statement. It's got her nasty trotters stamped all over it.'

'That's what I thought. I'm scared they'll run with it – the press, I mean. Especially if it's a quiet time for news. At least it's not in the nationals, but I need to keep my head down.'

'I totally understand. The *Morning Post* can make a story of a cat stuck in a tree stretch out for weeks. So this is massive news for them. I hate to say it, but they'll only lay off when there's another lead on the murder, or if a bigger story blows into town.'

Shuddering, I climbed back into bed. 'Oh, Gloria, I feel—'

'Helen.' Gloria's voice was firm. 'You've got me on your side. And I'm going to find the real killer.'

I wiped my eyes and sat up straight. 'No, Gloria. *We* are going to find the killer.'

'That's the spirit.'

'I've got no choice. Best if we don't involve Jade, though. She's too young to drag into all this.'

'You're probably right. She's a bit distracted, anyway. Boyfriend trouble, I believe.'

Gloria insisted we needed to speak to Tia-Marie, and I reminded her that the awful Ryan seemed to know the girl.

'Let's hope he comes into the diner soon, and I'll wring it out of the scroat.'

'In the meantime, I'll check his Facebook account,' I said. 'It's a long shot, but Tia-Marie might be a 'friend', possibly under a different name?' At least it was something I could do from my room.

Gloria had infused me with energy and hope. After thanking her profusely and ringing off, I eagerly opened Ryan's Facebook profile. He'd not bothered with the privacy settings, and I scrolled through lad prank videos and boasts about his Xbox prowess.

No one resembling Tia-Marie popped up. She could be a friend of a friend. After trawling through Ryan's dubious mates for an hour, I threw down my phone in frustration. My neck ached, and I had a cramp in my hands.

Gloria didn't contact me again. I distracted myself by Googling empty commercial premises and houses in Buttersley. I had to focus on the future and give myself hope. This time, a modern, featureless box would do for a home. I'd poured all my love and attention into our cottage. Where had that got me? I was so over all that matching cushions business. My passion would go into the shop. I'd make it my life, and no one would be able to take it away from me.

By Tuesday afternoon, I was climbing the walls. To think, only days before, the hotel room had been my sanctuary. I pictured Gloria and Jade whizzing around the diner in their skates, while I was stuck there. I'd already chucked the day's *Morning Post* in the bin. Although in shreds, the headline still taunted me. 'No Further Suspects in the Doughnut Murder Case'.

Why hadn't Gloria rung? The diner would be busy, but even so, she could have sneaked a quick call or message. She hadn't replied to my tentative text. Perhaps Ryan hadn't been in yet, or maybe he'd nothing to tell? I paced the small room, glaring at my lifeless phone.

Maybe Gloria hadn't been serious, and she'd forgotten all about me? After all, we'd only been friends for a short while, and she had no obligations towards me. I seesawed from that dismal thought to one of wild optimism where Gloria would deliver the murderer before closing time. When the church clock struck six, I'd given up. Maybe I should go and stay with James after all?

She rang at seven. 'Sorry I couldn't call earlier, but I've only just finished work.'

How could I have doubted my friend? 'Poor you. Nearly a twelve-hour shift. You must be exhausted.'

'Helen, you wouldn't believe ... My feet are in tatters.'

I wanted to give her the chance to moan, but couldn't stop myself from asking about Ryan. In a weary voice, she told me he'd been nowhere near the place, and that line of enquiry was probably useless, anyway.

My heart sank. 'Sounds like you've given up?'

'Not at all.' She injected excitement into her voice. 'Who needs that little runt when I've found Tia-Marie all by myself?'

I could have bounced on the bed in delight. 'You never fail to surprise me. How did you manage it?'

She laughed. 'Well, it wasn't by any clever detective work. I had my hand down the toilet in the gents at the time.'

'What?'

'Cleaning it. Tracy's given that job to me, seeing as she's sacked you. I found Tia-Marie's business card on the floor, down by the U-bend.'

'Business card? What sort of business is she in?'

'Oh, Helen, love.' Gloria sighed. 'You're so naive. Guess?'

'She's not a—'

'Let's call her an escort. Bookings taken strictly through her agency, Kittens-in-Heels. According to her card, she's the cutest cat in town.'

'Meow.' My heart raced. 'I'll book her. Then we get to see her in person.'

'Okay. Text me.' Yawning, she added, 'I'll have to go now. I just want to grab a bite to eat and go to bed.'

Clicking on the escort agency's website, I almost fainted at the price of kittens. It would take a whole week's wages from Donny's to pay for an 'evening of fun' with Tia-Marie. More expense to H Chandler's card. Naming myself Harry, I booked a date for the following evening and texted Gloria the details.

Supply Chain Management

I spent 'Day Three of the Doughnut Murder Case' pacing the hotel room. In the space of three days, the walls had closed in, and the swirly pattern on the brown and orange carpet irritated me beyond all reason. At each turn, I glared at the generic beach scenes on the walls. The images had seared onto my eyeballs, and if I ever saw them anywhere else, I'd tear them down from the walls. The prospect of venturing outside made me sweat, but I couldn't wait to speak to Tia-Marie.

When the time came, I zipped up my jacket, pulled the hood over my curls, and placed my clammy palm on the door handle. It almost slid off. Fighting the urge to open the door inch by inch, I recalled a day at the seaside with James. Flapping around in the shallows, we dared each other to plunge headfirst into the North Sea waves. Summoning that same grit, I braced myself and yanked open my door.

No one paid me the slightest attention in the foyer or in the quiet streets as I hurried to the venue. By the time I sat huddled in a corner of the Mixy bar next to Gloria, my shoulders had relaxed, and I no longer gritted my teeth.

Tia-Marie glided in like a modern-day goddess. All dolled up in a tight red dress for her date with Harry, I almost felt gratified by the effort she'd made. The crowd of men hanging around the brightly lit bar parted in awe.

Gloria beckoned her over, and the girl hesitated. A tiny frown marred the smoothness of her brow. She didn't move. I waved and plastered an inviting smile on my face.

She walked uncertainly towards us. 'Sorry, but I'm supposed to be meeting someone.' Puckering her brow, she added. 'Do I know you from somewhere?'

'Maybe if we were wearing roller skates, you'd recognise us?' said Gloria. 'Donny's Diner – the opening party?'

'How could I forget?' She pulled her perfect cupid's bow down in distaste. 'Nice to see you again, but as I said, I'm meeting—'

'Harry,' I said. 'That's us. We've booked you.'

Her hazel eyes popped behind the dense black lashes. 'I don't usually do girl on—'

'No!' I protested so loudly, the men at the bar looked over. Lowering my voice, I said, 'Sorry, we just wanted a chat with you about the party. Won't you sit down and have a drink?'

She remained standing. 'What about the party? I gave a statement to the police. Why should I talk to you?'

Gloria stiffened at my side. We'd not considered that Tia-Marie might be uncooperative. With breathtaking arrogance, I thought I'd bought her.

'Have a drink at least.' I poured a glass of Prosecco. 'Treat it as a night off.'

She narrowed her eyes for a moment and shrugged. 'Okay, if you put it like that. Maybe just the one.' She draped herself on a seat. 'I don't usually drink while working.'

I smiled. 'Very sensible. I noticed you stuck to water at Donny's.'

'Got to keep your wits about you in my game.'

Gloria rose. 'But you can relax with us. I'll get another bottle.'

As we waited for Gloria to return, I thought it best to be candid. 'Sorry if you think we've got you here under false pretences, but the agency was our only means of contacting you, and ... I'm desperate.'

Tia-Marie raised her finely arched brows. 'Oh?'

'Perhaps you don't know, but I found Graham's body and was arrested for his murder.'

She edged back in her seat and widened her lovely eyes. 'You're the one in the news. I recognise you now.'

Thanks. 'The police released me, but I'm still under suspicion until they find the real murderer. It had nothing to do with me.'

She put down her glass. 'You say that, but how do *I* know? I want to keep out of all this. The agency said that any association with the murder could affect my bookings.'

'Really?' said Gloria as she plonked the ice bucket onto the table. 'If anything, I'd have thought it would enhance them.'

I jumped on Gloria's train. 'Yeah, it could only add to your allure. The mysterious *femme fatale*.'

'Actually, one of the other girls said something like that. Thought she was being bitchy.'

'Probably just jealous,' I threw in for good measure.

Gloria topped up our glasses. 'I suppose in a glamorous job like yours, there's bound to be jealousy and back-biting?'

Flicking her silky mane with both hands, Tia-Marie leaned back and exposed the outline of her magnificent breasts. 'Jealousy! The word doesn't cover it.' With a complacent smile, she added, 'The ones that don't get much work are the worst.'

'That won't be you, then,' I said. 'I bet you've got plenty of clients. Do you have many regulars?'

She nodded. 'When I choose to see them. This is just part-time to get me through uni.' She pulled herself up straight. 'I'm doing my doctorate.'

'Oh,' I said. 'What in?'

'Supply chain management.'

What?

Gloria gave a low whistle. 'Wow. I'm impressed.' As the girl preened like an overfed cat, Gloria casually asked, 'Was Graham a regular?'

'No.'

This was going to be harder than we'd thought. I grabbed the bottle. 'Have another drink. Graham seemed pleasant enough, but you appeared to have your work cut out?'

'God, he was such a bore. I wondered why he'd booked me until I spotted that old frump giving me daggers. Thought it might have something to do with her.' She drained her glass. 'Cheers. Actually, this *does* make a nice change from having another God's gift to women groping me all night.'

Gloria finished her drink. 'Well, you've got to admit, the party turned out anything but boring. Women jealous of you yet again. Both Tracy and Pauline seemed to have it in for you.'

Trying not to laugh at Gloria's unsubtle approach, I spluttered out my drink. 'Sorry, the bubbles went up my nose.'

Gloria ignored me. 'You must have been relieved when Graham sent you home in a taxi?'

'I suppose so, but ...' the girl pouted. 'Missed out on the extras money, didn't I? The stingy old sod. Mind you, I didn't fancy all that dandruff over my ...' She peered down at her cleavage. 'You know.'

We all shared a grimace. As we'd bonded so nicely, I judged it time to lob in a pertinent question. 'So, you'd not met Graham before, but am I right in thinking Donny was one of your regular clients?'

The Edifice Crumbles

Tia-Marie didn't flinch at my suggestion about Donny. 'Yeah, when I first started out a couple of years ago, he couldn't get enough of me.' She looked towards the bar. 'They do a decent cocktail here by the way.'

Gloria sighed and rose. 'I'll get the cocktail menu.'

'You were saying about Donny,' I said.

Tia-Marie smoothed down the front of her dress and smirked. 'His attentions paid for my first car.'

'But Donny didn't seem overjoyed to see you at the party. I suppose he was shocked you were with Graham?'

'Wasn't he just?' She sneered. 'He couldn't bear to see me with someone else.'

'Are we still talking about Donny?' asked Gloria as she returned with the menu.

Seizing it from Gloria's hand, Tia-Marie ran her finger down the list before tapping it with a crimson nail. 'I'll have a Between the Sheets.'

I handed my credit card to Gloria. 'Nothing for me, Glo. I've had enough. Get whatever you want.'

Without prompting, Tia-Marie continued, 'I had to cool it with Donny in the end. He was coming on too strong. Can you believe he actually thought we were an item?' She blew out her sun-kissed Maybelline cheeks. 'As if.'

I copied her action. 'What a self-deluded idiot. Why would you even consider it?'

Gloria plonked four cocktails on the table. 'Two-for-one deal. I got confused. You'll have to help us out, Helen.'

Tia-Marie leaned forward like an overzealous croupier and pulled two towards her. 'Never turn down a cocktail.'

'Good thinking,' I said. 'It seems that when Donny was chasing you, he was married to someone called Liz.'

'He might have been.' Tia-Marie removed the flamed orange peel from her drink and dropped it on the table. 'Men tell me such boring stuff – like I'm interested.'

'Did Graham say anything about this Liz?' I asked.

'He did, as it happens.'

My stomach flipped.

Gloria sucked loudly on her straw. 'Go on, T, you've got to tell us.'

Our escort friend wrinkled her pert little nose. 'There's such a thing as client confidentiality.'

'Well, Graham's dead,' I said. '*He* won't mind. My liberty's at stake, and you've no loyalty to Donny. He's no longer a client. You've already said you had to give him the heave-ho.' As she didn't appear to be wavering, I added, 'Actually, Donny was quite insulting about you at the party. It struck me at the time because it was petty and mean.'

She stabbed at the peel with her cocktail stick. 'Oh, I can believe it. Donny has another side. All that happy-chappie stuff's just a front. He's got a vicious temper and can be proper nasty. When I wanted to cool it with him, he complained to the agency and tried to get me sacked. Even said I'd stolen from him.'

'That's terrible,' I said.

Gloria nodded. 'Dirty old letch. I hope Graham was more of a gentleman. Wasn't he the brother of this wife of Donny's – Liz?'

Well done, Gloria, for getting us back on track.

'So he said.' Tia-Marie grabbed her second cocktail.

'Did Donny and Liz divorce?' I clapped a hand over my mouth as if struck by a thought. 'She didn't find out about you, did she? You said he saw your dating as a proper relationship.'

'No idea. He used to drone on and on about how much he hated her. She had loads of money from a previous marriage, but she wouldn't help with his business ventures. Probably saw how crazy they were. He joked about how he'd got her life insured. One day he'd be rich and whisk me away to paradise.' Our date gave a tiny burp. 'All the old ones say that.'

'Did you tell Graham all this at the party?'

Tia-Marie nodded. One of her false eyelashes had slipped, making her features slightly lopsided. 'Yeah. Speaking to him brought it all back. How Donny, that fat little nobody, tried to ruin my reputation. Graham showed a lot of interest at first, but then I could hardly get a word out of him.'

'I noticed Graham went quiet. Maybe you'd given him something to think about?'

She removed a strand of hair that had stuck to her lipstick. 'Whatevs.' Raising the glass to her smudged, shiny lips, she added, 'Cheers.' She downed the cocktail in seconds and placed the lipstick-stained glass back on the table. 'Aren't you drinking yours? I'll have it if you don't want it.'

I pushed it towards her.

'Ryan seemed to know you,' said Gloria.

'Don't talk to me about that moron.' Tia-Marie slammed her glass down so hard, some of the pink goo spilt out. She topped up the glass with the dregs of the Prosecco.

Gloria mopped up the mess on the table. 'I know. What a slimeball. You were at school with him?'

Tia-Marie's head fell forward. 'The skinny runt. None of the girls liked him. Any more of that plonk left?'

Gloria stood. 'I know my way to the bar. One glass of Prosecco coming up.'

Tia-Marie raised her head. 'Make it a bottle.'

I winced and handed my credit card over once more.

Tia-Marie's phone buzzed, and she held up her hand. 'Sorry, it's work.' She pulled a face at the phone. 'What? Him again? Old Cheesy-Wotsits breath. Okay, tomorrow at eight.'

When Gloria returned with another ice bucket and three coffees, I returned to the subject of Ryan. 'Do you think he could be violent? At the party, he nearly went for Graham with a broken bottle.'

Tia-Marie misjudged the distance to her mouth and spilt wine on her dress. As it trickled down the ravine of her breasts, she poured another glass. 'He had a real cruel streak. Know what he used to do?'

'Tell us in a minute,' I said. 'Have some water. What about a coffee?'

'I'm having a night off, aren't I?' She knocked back her wine and belched like a navvy. 'Oops. 'Scuse me. It's so flamin' gassy, this plonk. Where was I? Oh, yeah, that scroaty scumbag, Ryan. He used to trap insects in a jar. All creepy crawlies. Then he'd shake the jar like crazy and drop matches in it. Nutter or what?' Her mouth remained open, and a drop of spittle leaked out of one side.

'How cruel,' I said. 'That's horrible.'

Tia-Marie poked my shoulder. 'He did worse than that. My friend's sister caught him torturing a cat. Can you believe it? Personally, I reckon it's 'cause he's so weedy.'

'You could be right,' said Gloria in a weary voice.

'Hey, you two, is Ryan's fat girlfriend your boss? You should warn her about him. He's totes bad news, but ...' Tia-Marie hung her head and gulped. 'That one can probably look after herself.'

I couldn't think of any other questions after that, and Gloria had slumped in her seat. Tia-Marie reached for her phone, held it high and took some selfies. She smiled at the results, but they all looked blurred to me.

After another half hour, our date tossed the empty bottle into the bucket and lurched from her seat. 'Want to go home now. Where the hell's my bag?' She pulled at her hair, dislodging an extension. 'No thief better not have swiped it. It's Chanel.'

Gloria unhooked it from the back of Tia-Marie's chair. 'There you are. Now let's get you home.'

Leaving the Mixy bar, I naively thought we'd load Tia-Marie into a taxi and wave a cheerful goodbye. But stepping into the cold night air, she sank to her knees on the pavement.

After pulling her up, we stood like three stooges in the pouring rain, with Tia-Marie sagging between us. Several taxis drove past with the drivers shaking their heads. In the end, I had to leave her propped against Gloria in a doorway while I flagged one down.

With judgemental eyes, and his meter already running, the driver watched us drag a rain-sodden dead weight into the back. He swivelled as far as his belly would allow. 'You'll have to pay double if she's sick.'

'Well, don't drive like an idiot,' said Gloria, pushing at Tia-Marie's tight rear, 'and she'll be fine. What's your address, T?'

Tia-Marie spent most of the journey with her head hanging out of the window and hair streaming behind. By the time we arrived, it had spread wide like a thicket. Then she wouldn't budge from the back seat. 'Leave me here. I just wanna sleep.'

Squatting in his seat like an overweight Buddha, the driver refused to turn off the meter. 'Not my problem, love. Health and safety, innit? Not allowed to help the punters.'

We cajoled, we tugged, and we pulled, but nothing would shift the woman. When she started lashing out and screaming, we had to back off.

'If she's not out in two minutes,' warned the driver, 'I'm calling the police.'

Gloria snarled. 'I'm reporting you, you useless lump of lard.'

'You do that, love. Just doing my job.'

I had a brainwave. 'Tia-Marie, your lovely Chanel bag's fallen out onto the mud.'

Like a ferret after a rabbit, she shot out of the taxi.

I threw money at the driver, and he waved two fingers as he sped off.

'Have you got your door key, love?' asked Gloria.

Tia-Marie tipped her bag out on the path, and I poked around in the detritus of make-up and tissues. 'I can't see one.'

Gloria was peering at the buttons on the entry system. 'We could get someone to buzz us in. Who's likely to still be up, T?'

'Not Dave. He's a wan—'

'I'll try someone else.'

Fortunately, we got Katie, a student friend, who was staying up late to finish an essay. And she knew where Tia-Marie hid the spare key to her flat.

The job became easier once we manoeuvred our charge into the messy bedroom. I held back her hair as she threw up in a bin.

Gloria found a large glass and filled it with water. 'Drink this before you get into bed.'

After Tia-Marie gulped it down, we prised off the filthy sausage-skin dress and rolled her under the duvet. Finding a beaten-up teddy bear on the floor, I threw it in beside her. We left them tucked up together with the goddess sucking her thumb.

After locking the door, we slipped the key through the gap underneath. Gloria phoned for two taxis, which arrived almost immediately. I'd wanted to linger and discuss Tia-Marie's information, but my friend's sagging shoulders and drooping eyelids warned me away.

Back alone in my hotel room, I sat on the bed, hugging my knees. After such a long night, I'd been glad to crawl back, but I was too wired to sleep. Fragments of conversations, memories from the party, and the snippets disclosed earlier, darted like fireflies inside my head. Donny married to Liz, but running around with an escort and accusing her of theft when she didn't comply. Said he had his wife well-insured. Ryan burning insects and torturing cats. Graham going quiet at the party. Said he'd had his suspicions at the time. What had happened to Liz? Graham scribbling in a notebook. Donny bragging to Tia-Marie he'd be wealthy. Ryan ready to attack Graham with a bottle. Pauline, though married to Donny, seemingly jealous of Tia-Marie. She'd grabbed Graham's lapels and slapped him.

As the church clock struck three, I poured boiling water onto a sachet of Belgian chocolate and took it back to bed. Cradling my hands around the steaming mug, I made my plans for the next day. Emboldened by my outing, I intended to catch a train.

Liz Online

Those fireflies continued to dart, and I couldn't sleep.

Gloria's phone call woke me at six. 'I can't be on for long,' she said. 'I've slept in. Slept like the dead.'

'Lucky you. I've been up all night going over what Tia-Marie told us.'

'Jeez, that girl could drink. I thought it was never going to end.'

'I feel guilty about encouraging her. I only meant it to be an icebreaker.'

'You didn't force it down, and it certainly made her spill the beans about Donny.'

'And all that stuff about Liz – the second wife.'

'Yeah, I know. No wonder Tia-Marie grabbed Graham's interest. Sounds like she revealed stuff about his sister's marriage he didn't have a clue about.'

'Must be why he went quiet,' I said. 'He needed to think. But why would that get him killed?'

'Listen, I've got to go, or I'll be late.'

'Bye then, Glo—' I was going to say we needed to discover what happened to Liz, but my friend had already gone.

The three wives of Donny. Number one must have been Tracy's mother. What had happened to her? Did he divorce both his former wives? And it appeared his marriage to Pauline was turning sour. Not a great track record.

But who was I to judge? Barely thirty, and I already had one failed marriage under my belt. I rested my head against the pillows and reflected on the course of relationships. How can love be so blissfully easy at first but then go so horribly wrong?

I touched the globe and thought about Zack. Trying not to dwell on his rejection, I focused on when we first met. James had invited me to stay at his student squat. I bumped into Zack in the kitchen and marvelled that such a bronzed Adonis was frying fish fingers.

Madly in lust and love, we married within two years. Prue said I was far too young and immature. What did *she* know? I couldn't imagine she'd ever experienced such intensity of feeling. My only reservation: James had gone travelling and couldn't make the wedding. We could have waited, but I sometimes wondered if we both feared he might talk us out of it.

Four hours after my phone call with Gloria, I sat in a cafe near Leeds station, enjoying a full English breakfast. My train would leave in twenty minutes. I'd already phoned Prue. I'd wanted to surprise her by turning up unannounced, armed with her favourite cherry liqueurs. But I needed to know if any of the *Morning Post* reporters had been sniffing around in Buttersley and asking about me.

If she was delighted at the prospect of my visit, she disguised it well. 'It's my day for the butcher's, so you'll have to meet me in town. What? No, no one's been asking about you. We've had no strangers here.'

Since I first left home, Northern Dash had modernised their trains. Garish colours replaced the brown dowdiness. It was like comparing Pauline to Tia-Marie. I preferred the comfortable old ones with the faded prints on the walls.

I leaned back, peered through the window, and a thrill of adventure shot through me. I did one of Gloria's snorts. Zack was possibly rattling along on the Trans-Siberian Express, and there was I, travelling not twenty miles to my hometown.

Though close to the city, Buttersley, with its unspoilt elegance and quieter ways, belonged to a different era. A lump formed in my throat as I searched for the first view of the moor. Nearer the station, the familiar municipal buildings came into view, magnificent as ever in their local Millstone Grit. Buttersley had always punched high. Prue could live in no other place.

As I stepped down from the train, my phone pinged with a message from Gloria.

Tracy's popped out, so we're putting our feet up. Jade looked up Liz online. She's sent you a link.

After opening Jade's attachment, I stood stock-still on the platform as people tutted and dodged around me. The fate of Liz had intrigued me, but I'd never expected that.

Love to the Beehive

Liz Donoghue had been killed two years ago in a hit-and-run. The driver had never been found.

After the initial shock, I wished I'd not read the attachment. There was nothing I could do about it then, but it would nag away at me all the same. And I'd wanted to devote my day to Buttersley and Prue.

The crowd bumped me along to the station exit, and I emerged blinking into the sunlight. It was one of those exceptionally cold, crisp days of winter when the habitual grey sky reverts to a brilliant, but surprising, clear blue.

Attempting to cross the busy road outside, I swore at the cars hurtling past. Had it been on a road like this where Liz met her death? I jumped back as a van sounded its horn, and the man inside glared.

With twenty minutes to spare before meeting Prue, I headed towards the high street, where the shops had barely changed since my childhood. New ventures occasionally appeared on the side roads, but they never lasted long. The high street was the only place to be.

I hoped one of the interiors might be empty with a 'To Let' sign in the window. But Prue would surely have told me. My unrealistic hopes were soon crushed by reality.

I examined the shops with a newly critical eye. The Wise Owl Bookshop had done well out of my pocket money. I spent most Saturday mornings in the children's section on a wobbly red chair with a pile of books on my knees. My mum had to bribe me away with the promise of ice cream. A display of books by a local author took up most of the window. She'd made it big in the world of crime fiction, and The Owl boasted signed copies and dagger-shaped bookmarks.

Klondike Estates hadn't changed, but it had a new neighbour – The Ruby Slipper. The shop front gleamed with fresh paint and it had a classy-looking sign. Stopping to admire their display of patent boots, I thought I might pop in later.

Clutterbuck's Hardware stood on Klondike's other side. Cruel-looking metal tools, dangerous saws, and pliers hung in the window. Faded handwritten price tags dangled over a graveyard of wasps.

Further down the row, past the charity shops, I half expected Prue to be in the butcher's, complaining about the size of cutlets. I popped my head around the door.

'Mrs Mayflower's been and gone,' said Mr Bassington, wiping spade-like hands on his apron. 'Anyway, love, nice to see you. I hope you're keeping well.'

'I'm fine, thanks. Your new canopy looks very smart.'

He beamed and lifted his straw hat. 'And so it should.' He chuckled. 'Cost more than a side of beef, did that.'

I fancied a canopy for my shop. That's if my dreams ever materialised. I was perhaps deluded in thinking I could start straight away in a premium spot. I might have to take my chances on the side streets.

Not wanting to be late for Prue, I rushed past Bright Sparks Electrics. They'd not changed their display since I was twelve, and the bulbs in the dated lamps barely glowed through the dust. What a waste of a grand, elegant window.

I wished she hadn't suggested meeting outside the barber's. As a child, the sign in the window had dominated my nightmares. It wasn't so much the grinning, disembodied faces that had scared me, but the tagline above. 'We need your heads to do our business.' I couldn't imagine what they did in there.

My heart tugged at the first sight of Prue. Smart and snug-looking in her fur-collared dogtooth coat, she was consulting her watch; no doubt hoping to chastise me for being a minute late.

I crept up beside her. 'Boo!'

She started and clutched the box-style handbag close to her chest. 'You big, silly dope. You could have given me a heart attack.'

I'd not seen her in almost a year. Apart from more grey streaks in her beehive and a few additional fine lines, Prue looked much the same.

I'd long since towered above her. 'Come here, you old battleaxe.' I scooped her into my arms and was rewarded by a whiff of the familiar gardenia and rose petal scent.

Since I turned fourteen, Prue was all I'd known as a mum. And despite her prickly nature, she'd always done her best for me. Besides, Mrs Jones – James's mum – was usually there to dish out the treats behind Prue's rigid back.

'Mind my hair. I've just had it done.'

She pecked my cheek, and I made a note to scrub it later. Prue bought her plum-coloured lipstick in bulk from a chemist's in the Dales. James maintained it was brewed in a cauldron from bats' blood and cement.

'Lovely to see you, Prue.' I pointed to the bag at her feet. 'Do you want me to carry that? It looks heavy.' Bending down to lift it, I groaned. 'What's in here? A ton of bricks?'

'In a sense, yes.' She couldn't hide a proud little smile. 'It's full of brochures from all the local estate agents. Mr Klondike was particularly helpful.' She glanced at me from the corner of her eye. 'That's if you're serious about coming back to live here?'

'How thoughtful.' I didn't have the heart to say I could find it all online. 'And yes, I'm serious about coming back.'

The beam she returned lifted my heart, and for the first time in months, I felt wanted and loved.

I linked my arm in hers. 'So, where are you taking me? We're just in time for elevenses. What about Rita's Rolls?'

Prue's snort rivalled Gloria's best. 'I would not be seen dead in—'

'Only joking.' I squeezed her arm as we passed Rita's steamed-up window. Everything they sold was fried and served in a white, claggy roll. We used to pile in after school. Their bacon sandwiches were to die for.

'I could always tell when you'd been in there, my girl. You used to come home reeking of chip fat.'

I stopped at an A-frame sign on the pavement. It showed a cartoon-style hand pointing down the side street. 'That's new. Planet Pitta. Shall we go there?'

Prue pursed her lips and shook her head. 'No. Betty and I tried it last week. Never again. At my time of life, I see no reason to drink something called chai out of a tin mug.'

'Can I just have a look? See how it's decorated?'

'You don't need to look. I can save you the bother. It's got flour sacks on the walls. Sacks? I ask you. The tables are all mismatched and scuffed. And the chairs ...' Prue shuddered, 'the chairs are metal. They did nothing for Betty's back.'

'Mmm, I get the picture. That's trendy, Prue.'

'Well, I don't like it. We had to queue at the counter. Can you believe there's no waitress service? As for the coffee ...' She put a hand to her head. 'A boy, far too young to have a beard, lectured us for a full five minutes on where they got their coffee from, how long he'd trained, and the specifications of their over-large machine. "Just give me a spoonful of Nescafé", said Betty as soon as she could get a word in. That shut him up.'

My phone pinged in my pocket.

'So, it'll have to be the Doily Carte.' I sighed. 'Buttersley's just crying out for a decent tea room.'

'Then you'd better get your skates on, my girl.'

Prue could not have known the horrors she'd just conjured up. I was so glad my skating days were over. Gloria and Jade would be whizzing around as we spoke.

We pushed open the gilded door of the tea room, and the cloying warmth hit me in the face. While removing our coats, I sneaked a look at my phone. I'd received a message from Gloria.

Trouble at Donny's. It's all kicking off here.

Donny's Diner and the Doily Carte were worlds apart. Forget the roller skates; at the Doily, the waitresses shifted like snails. Margaret, an ogre of a woman in serge, ran the show from behind a fortress of a cash desk. At her command post next to the door, she didn't miss a thing. Lack of competition meant the place was always busy, but the food was dull and the atmosphere oppressive.

A scruffy handwritten sign ordered us to wait until allocated a table. Prue pointed at the empty tables and tutted loudly. 'Come on, you rabbit. What are you waiting for? We'll sit in the window.'

Conscious of Margaret stalking our progress, I meekly followed my leader. At any moment, I expected to be felled by an arrow in my back.

Once seated, Prue smiled serenely at Margaret, nodded at acquaintances and gave the odd regal wave. 'Are the scones fresh today?' she asked the waitress.

'Yes, Mrs Mayflower.'

'I'll have my usual, then.'

The waitress slowly scrawled on her pad and turned to me.

'Could I have a skinny latte, please, with an extra shot?'

'A what, love?'

Prue sniffed. 'She's been living in London. A milky coffee will do.'

As the waitress ambled away, I surveyed the dark-panelled room. Toby jugs and novelty teapots stood on paper doilies and competed for space on the oak dresser. Faded placemats depicting scenes from 'ye olde England' covered our table, and splinters from the hard seat had already snagged my tights.

'I don't mean to boast, Prue, but I could do better than this in *my* tea room.'

Prue nodded her beehive and smiled. 'You've always had a flair for design.'

That was all the encouragement I needed to prattle on about my plans. 'I want to create a stunning but welcoming environment with marble-topped tables, sparkling chandeliers, and Lloyd Loom chairs. We'll serve coffee from the best Arabica beans, and the food will be fresh and homemade.' Prue appeared to be interested, so I continued. 'I'd like premises with two rooms, where the customers would walk through the shop section to access the tea room. Can you imagine, Prue, glass cabinets full of Belgian truffles, patisserie, and displays of exquisitely packaged confectionery from around the world?'

'Very nice, dear. Speaking of premises, I may have some news for you on that front. But I can't say any more at the moment, so don't ask. I'm just popping to the ladies.'

It wouldn't do to get my hopes up. As soon as she left the table, my thoughts returned to the implications of Liz's death. As a distraction, I sneaked a look at my phone. No more messages from Gloria, but one from Jade popped up.

The police are here! That Constable Harper's sooooo cute.

'Apparently, the police are at the diner,' I told Prue when she returned. 'They might have a new lead.'

'It sounds like a dreadful place. How could you have got yourself mixed up in all that? The *Morning Post* has been quite shocking. I've got a good mind to put in a complaint. Luckily, no one *here* knows your married name.' She cut into her anaemic-looking scone and sighed. 'These don't get any better. And staying in a hotel. What a waste. I want you to come back to Buttersley. Your bedroom's just as you left it. It's no longer messy, of course.'

I scraped the skin off my grey-looking coffee. 'That's so kind of you. And I might take you up on it, but for now, I want to stay in Leeds until this murder business is sorted. Might be sooner rather than later if they've found a new suspect.'

'Well, the offer's there.' She patted her beehive. 'And don't feel obliged, thinking it's for my benefit. I'm not a lonely old bat who needs the company.'

I laughed. 'That never crossed my mind. It would certainly be handy living with you while I'm looking for somewhere more permanent.'

'If you made a shortlist from those brochures, I could inspect them first. Possibly even take Betty along for a second opinion.' Despite her casual tone, Prue couldn't hide her enthusiasm.

Should I have been touched by her eagerness to facilitate my return, or did she just fancy being nosy? Maybe a little of both. In any case, I was happy for her to take on that role, as I had zero interest in house interiors.

'That would be great, thanks.' My money should be coming through from the sale of the cottage any day soon.'

'It is none of my business, but ...' A delicate flush appeared on Prue's cheeks, and she leaned in closer. 'Will you have enough money?'

I smiled. 'I should have. The cottage was in my name only. The apartment in Zack's. So, there should be enough equity to buy a modest house and launch a business.' I crossed my fingers. *That's if I don't carry on spending like an idiot.*

Prue nodded and sat back. As she waved at an acquaintance, my phone rang. I couldn't resist taking a peek.

It could be Gloria with more news from the diner. I looked at Prue. 'It's James. Do you want to speak to him?'

She shrugged but didn't say no.

'Hi, James. Putting you on loudspeaker. I'm having a coffee in the Doily with Prue.'

'Thought I could feel the heat of a dragon's breath on my neck.'

Prue bristled. 'I'll give you what for, young man.'

'I've conjured a charming image,' he said, 'of you both nestling amongst the Toby jugs.'

She tutted. 'Are you wearing one of your ridiculously loud shirts?'

'Of course. I must have known I'd have the pleasure of talking to you today. I'm wearing a pink and green Versace Barocco. Now it's your turn. Tell me what *you're* wearing.' He laughed. 'I didn't expect to be involved in one of these sorts of conversations so early in the day.'

Prue glared at my phone, and I almost expected it to combust. 'Don't be so ridiculous,' she said. 'And shouldn't you be working?'

'As always, Prue, your finger is on the pulse. The truth is, commerce bores me, and I'd far rather be exchanging pleasantries with you.'

'Well, if you're so bored, you might want to call your mother. I saw her yesterday buying her Finny haddock. She said she'd not heard from you in weeks.'

I glanced around. Our neighbours had suspended their conversations. Prue had raised her volume as if conversing with a figure on top of a skyscraper.

Let them listen. In a three-way chat with my two favourite people, I'd forgotten all my troubles. 'Hey, James, did you ring for any particular reason?'

'Just checking in. All sweet with you?'

'Apart from this dreadful scone,' said Prue.

A little self-conscious now, I told James there had been developments at the diner and I'd ring him later.

'Okay. Love to the beehive. Bye.'

Prue automatically touched her hair. 'That boy's always had too much cheek. Mr and Mrs Jones must be constantly asking themselves where they went wrong.'

After the Doily, we took advantage of the sunny day and walked around the park. I bought us a takeaway coffee each, and we sat in the bandstand for over an hour.

Eventually, I parted from Prue with reluctance. Maybe she felt the same way, as she allowed me to hug her without resisting. As I trudged towards the station with my heavy bag of brochures, a strange mixture of sorrow and optimism shot through me.

Gloria rang while I was on the train, but the signal was poor, and I just about heard every other word.

'We've been ...'

'What?'

'Donny's ... and ... all shocked.'

I could have thrown my phone through the window. 'This is ridiculous. Can you hear me?'

'Just about ... been arrested.'

'Who's been arrested?'

The call ended. Sighing, I texted to ask if she was still in the city centre. I'd be arriving in fifteen minutes, and did she want to meet me at the station?

She replied with a thumbs-up.

You Murderers Are All the Same

Gloria and Jade were waiting at the ticket barrier. They linked my arms and declared they were dying for a drink.

'So what's been going on?' I asked as we hurried to the nearest bar.

'The police came just before eleven,' said Jade. 'We were really busy, and I didn't even notice them at first. Dracula and Constable Harper again. And guess what?'

'Gloria said something on the phone about—'

Jade tapped my arm. 'Think he's going to ask me out.'

'What? Who?' I asked.

'Constable Harper.'

Gloria snorted. 'Yep, that's the crucial bit, Jade's love life. Apart from Pauline being arrested, of course.'

'What?' I stopped in my tracks. A man bumped into my back and swore.

'Told you it'd be one of the Donoghues, didn't I?' said Gloria. 'That lets *you* off the hook.'

I would have expected relief to wash over me, but I only felt numb. I pictured Pauline at the police station going through the same processes as me. She might even be lying on that hard, blue bench in my old cell. She'd be scared, lonely, and in need of a solicitor. I would never have pegged her as a murderer.

We entered the warmth of the Fahrenheit Bar, and I sank gratefully onto a red velvet-padded seat in a high-sided booth. Gloria flopped beside me.

Jade remained standing. 'I expect you two oldies want me to go to the bar?'

Gloria handed over a twenty. 'Less of your cheek, young pup. Gin and tonic for me – a double if it's happy hour – and whatever you two want.'

'Same for me, Jade. Thanks.'

Gloria sat back, removed her shoes, and massaged her feet. 'The Donoghues are really going to struggle at the diner. Pauline's the only one with any idea how to run the place.'

'I can't believe she murdered Graham. I'd much rather it were someone like Ryan.'

'He wouldn't have the balls.'

We sat in silence for a moment. Perhaps, like me, Gloria was trying to erase unedifying images of Ryan from her head.

Breaking our reverie, Jade plonked our drinks on the table. 'Move up, you two. Let me in.'

Gloria seized a glass. 'Here's to your freedom, Helen.'

We all clinked glasses and took a long drink.

A nagging doubt persisted. 'But what if they've arrested the wrong person *again*? I might soon be back as the favoured suspect.'

Jade shook her head. 'Don't think so. Not from what Matt told me.'

'*Matt?*' we exclaimed.

Jade placed a hand on her chest and gave a smug smile. 'Constable Harper. I didn't tell you before, Glo. Thought I'd wait till we were all together.'

'Go on, then,' said Gloria, poking her in the ribs. 'What did he tell you?'

'He swore me to secrecy, but they found Pauline's fingerprints on the knife.' Jade leaned towards me. 'As well as yours. Also, a witness saw Pauline leave the building in the early hours of the morning.'

I gasped. 'Who was the witness?'

Jade shrugged. 'Matt couldn't say.'

Gloria stirred her drink. 'That's not exactly conclusive evidence, though. Wonder if they've got anything else?'

'I don't get why she'd do it?' said Jade. 'She seemed pretty friendly with Graham. Like she looked up to him.'

After hardly anything to eat, my head buzzed with the gin. 'Gloria overheard them arguing. Pauline was jealous of Tia-Marie, and Graham was pretty nasty to her about it.'

'Yeah, but ...' Jade scrunched up her face. 'Jealous of old dandruff head. Yuk. Oldies emoting all over the place is well gross.'

Gloria cuffed the back of Jade's head.

'How did the Donoghues take it?' I asked.

'Totes shocked, weren't they, Glo?'

'Yeah. Tracy went white as a sheet when the police walked in, and Donny looked like he'd been force-fed one of his own hot dogs. Ryan seemed unfazed and even smirked when they took Pauline away.'

'In handcuffs,' said Jade. 'Just like they did with you, Helen.'

'Thanks for reminding me. What happened then?'

Gloria drained her drink. 'It all went haywire after that. We struggled through lunchtime service, and then the Donoghues decided to close for the rest of the day. Said they needed to have an emergency meeting. Can't see the place lasting, myself. They definitely need more staff.'

They both leaned towards me, their faces flushed and eyes all bright and sparkly.

I shifted in the seat. 'What?'

They exchanged a glance.

'You could come back,' said Jade in a forced sing-song way. 'Couldn't she, Glo,' she added, enunciating her words as if speaking English for the first time.

Gloria snorted. 'Jade, you're not exactly subtle. I thought we were going to work up to that. Get us another drink, please. I need the loo.'

I handed over my credit card and watched my friends push through the throng. They'd forced me to consider my next move. Staying at the hotel would eat into my money. I should leave and go stay with Prue. That would be the rational thing to do. But despite the gin and the bright, busy bar, an indefinable unease niggled away. Maybe it was just hunger. Our booth was next to the dining area, and the heady mix of garlic, melted cheese and bacon made my stomach rumble. I was so hungry, I could almost have tackled one of Donny's hot dogs. That brought me back to my friends' suggestion.

I rounded on them when they returned. 'Is this your idea for me to come back, or have the Donoghues put you up to it?'

'Well,' said Gloria, 'let's just say, Donny always had a soft spot for you.'

Jade put down her phone and sighed. 'Don't you think he might have texted me by now, Glo?'

Gloria winked at me. 'Why would Donny be texting you?'

'Don't be silly.' Jade pouted. 'You know who I mean.'

'Harper? Give him a chance. He's probably still working out how to use his phone.'

I waggled my hands. 'Ahoy there, Love-Islanders. Thought we were talking about me?'

'Oh, yeah,' said Jade. 'I know Tracy said she wouldn't have you back at any price, but she is kinda desperate.'

'Thanks.'

'The thing is, Helen,' Gloria placed her hands over mine as if to deliver bad news, 'we need you. No one else can work that coffee machine.'

'I'll think about it, but—'

Jade clapped her hands. 'Fab. We'll all be back together. The dream team. Can't wait to see you back on your skates.'

'I haven't agreed yet. Actually, the more I think about it, the more ridiculous it seems. Don't forget that those bloody Donoghues threw me to the wolves. Not only did they release my photo and details to the press, but they made out that I was some sort of loser. A "misfit", they called me.' I leapt to my feet. 'How bloody dare they?'

The men at a table nearby slammed down their pints and cheered. 'You tell 'em, love.'

Gloria pulled me back down. 'Okay, don't get your knickers in a twist. What if the Donoghues apologise?'

'No. Not on your roller skates. Never!'

We broke up our party not long after that. Jade and Gloria had homes to go to, and I had a hotel room waiting for me.

Gloria squeezed my hand as we parted. 'Seriously, though, think about coming back to Donny's. We need you.'

Jade kissed my cheek. 'And don't worry about Tracy saying you're useless.'

'Thanks, Jade. I won't.' That did it. I had no intention of going back.

My hotel room, though stifling, was reassuringly familiar. And how could I fail to appreciate a warm, tidy room with fresh sheets on a king-size bed? I could be shivering in a filthy bedsit in Ampsley, or squashed in my teenage bedroom at Prue's. If staying at the hotel was my best option, I resolved to negotiate a discount. That's what a budding businesswoman would do.

After ordering a deep-pan pepperoni pizza with extra cheese, I tipped Prue's bag of house brochures onto the bed. I'd made a cup of tea and was about to flick through them when James rang.

'You've survived the Doily and Prue, then?'

I smiled. 'Oh, James, it was so lovely to go back. Prue's even offered to put me up until I find a house. But the thing is—'

'Isn't she worried you'd bring trouble to her door – as my mother would say – with all this murder business?'

'There's been a development. Pauline – that's Donny's wife – has been arrested for the murder, and they want me to go back to the diner.'

'Whoa! Slow down. Who does? You can't go back there.'

His assertive tone made me rebel. 'I'm considering it.'

'You fool. Are you mad?'

'I only said I was considering it.'

'But why would you want to return? They've treated you abysmally. You've no loyalty there. I can't believe—'

'Okay, okay. Don't go on.' He was right, but the disdain in his voice irritated me. 'I'm not rich like you. I need to work. My money hasn't come through, and I've got to live.'

'I'd pay for you *not* to work there.'

Though well-intentioned, that infuriated me. 'I don't need your charity.'

'The offer remains, my proud little pumpkin.'

I mumbled a graceless thanks. 'I'm a big girl, and I don't need you to bail me out. You know I've always worked and supported myself – even when living with Zack. Have you heard from him, by the way?'

James gave the same answer as always. A big fat no. 'Why don't you look for a job elsewhere while you're waiting to start your business?'

'Are you forgetting my name's been plastered all over the *Morning Post* these last few days? "The Hunt For Helen Merang", remember? Who in their right mind would employ me?'

James used his airy, dismissive tone. 'I wouldn't worry about that. No one takes any notice. Not in the sort of unskilled jobs you'd be chasing, anyway.'

I gripped the phone. How dare the golden boy of global investments talk down to me from his ivory tower? To *me*, who could still remember his snotty, playground nose. Not to mention the embarrassing accident in his trousers when the pantomime villain hissed too loudly. I reverted to the language of our childhood. 'Who do you think you are? Just get lost, will you.'

Throwing my phone on the bed, I cursed all men, or at least those closest to me. James and Zack always thought they knew best, viewing me as the little woman who knew nothing of life. James might be super-successful, living in one of his three Canary Wharf penthouse apartments, and Zack might be travelling the world, but I had ... God, what did I actually have? I pressed my face into my hands.

Maybe I should take up Prue's offer and stay with her, but that would be too much of a cop-out. I needed to see this through. My own shop in Buttersley would be a fresh start, and I didn't want my new future to be tainted by this murder business. The police needed to inform me, preferably in writing, that I was totally innocent. Maybe I should get Leticia on to that.

After demolishing my pizza and watching a rerun of *The Sweeney*, I slipped into bed with a mint-flavoured hot chocolate in hand. The regret over my churlish behaviour towards James nagged away. Despite his condescending attitude, he'd only been trying to help. I wouldn't be able to sleep if I didn't apologise.

Sighing, I reached for my phone. A text would probably work best. We'd only get into further confrontation if we spoke.

Sorry for being a touchy, childish cow. Big hugs and kisses.

He replied in seconds.

You murderers are all the same. Go whistle for a kiss.

Satisfied, I pulled the duvet around me.

A knock on the door woke me the next morning. My newspapers had arrived. I'd slept badly and could easily have rolled over and gone back to sleep, but curiosity made me crawl out of bed.

Poor Pauline. Whoever had supplied those terrible photos had done her no favours. They'd possibly been photoshopped, but the accentuated hook in her nose transformed her into the Wicked Witch of the East. One image showed her and Graham together. Reaching a hand up towards him, she could have been clawing out his eyes.

The Sun revelled in this gift of a story. Under 'A Sweet Affair Gone Wrong', the article detailed the relationship between Pauline and Graham, as if the writer had shared the very same bed.

The *Morning Post* didn't fail to annoy, and I cringed at the feebleness of its pun. 'I Dough-not Love You Any More'.

My sympathy for the woman didn't spoil my immense relief at no longer being a subject of interest. Helen Merang had slipped into obscurity, where she belonged.

Stretching out the story, the *Morning Post* dedicated a lengthy paragraph to 'The Devoted Doughnut King. A Life Now in Crumbs'. Where did they find those writers?

Their picture showed a dejected-looking Donny in a dark, well-cut suit. Taken from a flattering angle, the photo hid the belly and increased his height. Even his moustache was on point and conveyed a quiet dignity.

He appeared slightly younger, with maybe a touch more hair and fewer chins. The thought suddenly occurred that this may have been taken at the funeral of his second wife, Liz.

My phone rang, and I jumped at the name displayed. The man himself was on the line. What could Donny want with me? My finger hovered. I couldn't make up my mind whether to speak to him or to delete Donny's Diner forever.

A Man and His Dreams

I stared at my phone, suspicious of what Donny might want. The best course of action would be to heed James's advice, reject the call, and have nothing to do with the Donoghues.

No one could have been more surprised than me to hear from my lips, 'Good morning, Donny.'

'Hello, my darling. How are you?' He sounded far too chipper.

'Relieved I'm no longer "Hunted Helen". And I just want to clarify, Donny, I might be a "misfit" to your family, but I didn't steal those roller skates.'

'What? Oh, my sweet. We never said anything like that. As if we would. Banish that thought from your pretty little head. You know what journalists are like. They make things up. Me and my little Trace would never—'

Not a bit mollified, I cut him short. 'Just so you know, I donated them to charity. That's after spending all day locked up in a police cell.'

Donny spluttered. 'In my opinion, the police were far too precipitate. I said so at the time. My poor Tracy was inconsolable. Absolutely devastated when they took you away.'

I bet she was. After getting that off my chest, I'd nothing else to say.

'She's been my rock, has that girl,' he continued. 'I don't know how she does it. With all this carry-on, I need her even more.'

If he'd just rung to sing Tracy's praises, I would have to invent static on the line. 'Yes, I'm sure. It must be extremely difficult for you.' *Should I mention Pauline?*

'Helen, my lovely. You don't know the half of it. It's no exaggeration to say I'm a broken man.'

I pictured clumps of his moustache littering the floor like dead, shrivelled spiders.

I cleared my throat. 'Sorry to hear that.'

His next line threw me. 'Tell me, my darling, do you dare to have dreams?'

'Well, actually, yes, I—'

'Because I'm a man who's never been afraid to dream big, but the thing is ...' His voice trembled.

God, he's not going to cry, is he? After a moment of silence, I coughed. 'Er, I'm still here.'

'Just trying to gather my strength, dear.' He blew his nose. 'My dreams are in danger of being crushed by the cruel hand of fate. A malevolent force is working against me.'

What's he been watching on the telly? I half expected him to announce doughnut-destroying zombies were beating a path through Leeds city centre. Still no mention of Pauline.

'What do you mean? Are the police stopping you from opening the diner?'

I moved the phone away as Donny raised the decibels. 'The pigs wouldn't dare.' He spat out the last word, and his rapid shift from self-pity to rage startled me. He paused. 'No. We've decided to close the diner for a few days. Though we'll still be at it behind the scenes, of course. It's a weekend, and we'll lose our best days, but ...'

'Sounds like a good idea. Let the fuss die down.'

'Exactly, Helen, my darling. I knew you'd get it.'

Now would be the time to wish him every success on his reopening and end the call. 'Well, good luck, and I—'

'Helen, I need help.'

I recalled all that Tia-Marie had said about him turning nasty, and I steeled myself to be strong.

'We're desperately short of staff. No one has any loyalty these days.' His pleading tone turned to one of anger. 'It's just a job to them.'

Minimum wage for working like a dog. What else would it be?

His voice returned to its sugary setting. 'Thank God for those two angels, Gloria and ... and young what's her—'

'Jade.'

'Yes. Those two. They're like family to me. Gloria, so capable, and Jane, so quick on the skates.'

Jade, you berk. I forced a laugh. 'Then you won't want *me* back. I was useless on the skates.'

'But your coffee making was exemplary. And the way you commanded that counter. Well, I don't even think my Tracy could do better.' He gurgled a laugh. 'Don't you tell her I said that, mind.'

I tinkled an echoing laugh. 'Don't worry, I won't.' *I hope never to see her again.*

'It's about the staffing issue I've rung.'

I'm sure it is. Don't bother asking. I'm not coming back.

Donny's next words surprised me. 'The thing is, Pauline had arranged interviews for today. Not knowing ... obviously, that she'd be, er ...'

Arrested for murder?

He cleared his throat. 'Indisposed.'

I was fed up with this pussyfooting around. 'Donny, did you have no idea about Pauline ... about what she's supposed to have done? What motive did she have to kill Graham? She seemed quite fond of him.'

He sighed. 'No, love, I'd no idea.' Donny's voice lost its familiar bluster. 'It came as a terrible shock. But she's had her demons for a long time. In fact, she's never been the same since Tracy was ...'

'Since Tracy ...? Was what?' I prompted, certain that Donny had been about to say something important.

'Oh, that was years ago. All water under the bridge. Let's not talk about that. We've got a business to run. Unfortunately, my poor Tracy can't do the interviews at this sad time.'

'Is she too upset about Pauline's arrest?'

'What? No, it's not that.' He paused and said almost as an afterthought, 'Though she's very worried about Pauline, of course. Sadly, it's the anniversary of the death of my wife. It always takes my little Trace badly.'

'Oh, I'm sorry. Is that the death of Liz?'

'No. The sad passing of my first wife, Valerie. Tracy's, er ... mother,' he added as if he wasn't so sure. That didn't surprise me. With all those wives and their untimely deaths, he could do with a spreadsheet. 'It always hits her hard at this time of year, especially when she's only got her dear old dad.'

'Do you have any other children?'

'Regrettably, no. Valerie couldn't have—' He stopped abruptly. 'And, well, that's why my Tracy's so special.'

Donny said Tracy wanted him to do the job interviews. 'You know me, my lovely, I'm such a people person. But that's my problem: I see the best in everyone. Just one of my many little foibles.' He could not have squeezed more oil into his voice. 'So I thought you might ...'

'What? Do the interviews? *Me?*'

'Gloria said you had a fancy job in London working for an international bank. You'd be far better than me.'

Sighing in relief that he hadn't asked me to return as a speedy server, I considered his request. It wasn't like I'd anything better to do, and it might be good practice for my future business.

'Say no if you want, but you'll be rescuing a grateful, hardworking man who dares to have his dreams.'

I noted that he hadn't offered to pay me. 'I'll think about it.'

Donny might have read my mind. 'Obviously, I don't expect such quality services for free. I'll make it worth your while.' His voice turned triumphant as if he'd sealed the deal. 'I've got something special for you. What do you say?'

'I say we negotiate a fee.'

Lady Muck

It seemed strange to be back at the diner. Seeing it through fresh eyes, I could newly appreciate Donny's passion and vision. The gleaming black-and-white floor tiles contrasted with the red padded seats, the jukebox flashed, and sparkling lights bounced off the glass cabinets containing the vintage memorabilia. There was nothing else like it in Leeds.

My mood changed when my gaze fell on the coffee machine. Fingerprints and sticky marks defaced the chrome. I'd spent hours polishing that magnificent work of art, and my hand uncurled in my pocket, itching to grab a cloth. I wouldn't be able to leave without giving it a quick once-over – if not a full-scale clean and service.

The Drifters crooned in the background, but the place seemed deserted. After my first favourable impression, a sense of gloom descended, and despite the warmth of my heavy coat, I shivered. After all, Graham had been murdered there only one week before.

Fingers crossed, I hoped Gloria would be meeting me there later. I'd promised to treat her to steak and chips at her favourite restaurant.

'Thanks, Helen, I'd love that,' she'd said, 'but I've sort of half promised to call in at the in-laws. I'll see if I can change it to another day.'

I'd also invited Jade, but she was giddy about having a date with Constable Harper. 'We're meeting at City Square,' she'd cooed. 'Not far from you, so we might pop in to say a quick hello.'

Those loose arrangements would have to do, and I told myself off for being pathetic. I'd wanted my friends as backup. It was about time I stopped relying on their support.

The diner's Bakelite wall clock told me I'd arrived too early. Most of the tables had been pushed against the windows, but one remained in the middle with a notepad, jug of water and glasses on top. Two chairs stood at opposite sides.

'Hello. Donny, I'm here,' I called.

Silence. Even The Drifters had stopped.

I called out again. To my relief, a smiling Donny emerged from the kitchen. He hurried towards me with his flour-covered hands outstretched, and his moustache glittering with sprinkles.

'Just trying out a new topping,' he said. 'It keeps my mind off my troubles.' He swept his arm to the table. 'As you can see, I've set it all up for your interviews.' He beamed with pride as if he'd arranged summit talks for the world's most prominent leaders.

'Yes, very efficient. I'm a bit early. Shall I make us a coffee?' I could wipe down my precious baby at the same time.

'You've read my mind, darling. We've all missed your wonderful coffee. But before you do, allow me to present you with that very special gift I mentioned.' He picked up a box from the counter and thrust it towards me. 'It's my personal thank you for helping me out today.'

My arms sagged at the unexpected weight of the box. 'What does it contain, gold nuggets?' My voice sounded unnaturally high. Whatever it was, I didn't want a gift from Donny.

He shook his head, and multicoloured sprinkles flew in all directions. 'Something much more valuable.' His voice had turned reverential. He patted the box and smiled.

Intrigued, I ripped off the ribbons and tape. I'd never been able to open a gift in a dignified way. 'Oh, it's a pair of—'

'Nineteen-sixties roller skates. I knew you'd be thrilled. Proper metal they are, and real leather straps.' He balanced one in his hand. 'Feel the weight. None of that plastic rubbish Gloria and, er, Jane scoot around on.'

'Donny, that's so thoughtful and kind, but you shouldn't have wasted your money on me.'

He handed them over almost reluctantly. I hoped he didn't expect me to strap them on there and then.

'Such a shame I'm so useless on skates. But these are beautiful,' I added, not wanting to burst his bubble.

'A little memento for you, my dear. Think of me when you wear them.'

Hanging my head to hide my grimace, I placed them by the coffee machine.

The interviews took a couple of hours. Out of ten on the list, eight candidates showed up. Some even displayed lukewarm enthusiasm for the job, and apart from a couple of no-hopers, the rest would do. I was just writing a report for Donny when Tracy returned with scruffy Ryan in tow.

Tracy click-clacked towards me in her too-high heels. 'What the hell are *you* doing here?' She placed her fat little hands on the table and leaned into my space. Sour wine fumes wafted towards me, and her eyes blazed in a highly coloured face.

'Hello, Tracy. Nice to see you again. Been out for a drink, have you?'

'None of your business. Who d'you think you are? Sitting there like Lady Muck.'

I couldn't resist provoking her. 'Donny asked me to do the interviews. Thought you weren't up to it.'

Tracy's mouth dropped open, revealing small nicotine-stained teeth, clashing with the fuchsia lipstick. 'Liar. Dad would never say that.' She whipped her head around towards the kitchen. 'Dad!'

Ryan placed spider-tattooed hands over his ears. 'Steady on, Trace.'

Ignoring him, she hurried behind the counter.

I rose from my seat. 'Don't you think you should follow her, Ryan?'

Looking me up and down, he puckered his thin lips and kissed the air. 'Nah, I'd rather stay here and get cosy with you.' He moved to my side of the table. His body stank of stale perspiration and beer.

Not wanting to antagonise him, I forced a quick smile. 'I'd love to stop and chat, but I need the loo.' He planted his legs wide, and as I dodged around him, he anticipated my moves and blocked my escape. I tried to keep my voice calm. 'If you'd just let me pass.'

Grabbing my hair, he pulled my face closer to his. The blackheads on his greasy nose swarmed like tiny flies in front of my rapidly blinking eyes. As I jerked back, he drew me in tighter.

Telling myself he was nothing but a weedy bully, I bared my teeth and growled. 'Get out of my way or I'll punch you.'

He laughed. 'Love to see you try, darling.'

That did it. I summoned all my strength, lifted one end of the table and heaved the corner edge into his groin. Far more effective than just a knee. As he groaned, I pushed past and ran to the corridor. Safely on the other side of the door, I gulped for breath before realising my mistake. My stomach dropped. How could I have been such a fool? I'd left a well-lit cafe, visible to the street with shoppers bustling past, for a dark, secluded corridor. What if Ryan came after me?

The Truth Spills Out

I groped along the corridor wall for the light switch and was extremely relieved to make contact. But when I flicked it, nothing happened.

Trying not to panic, I turned to unzip my bag. The tiny but powerful beam of my phone's torch would soon sort me out. After a couple of seconds of clawing at nothing, I recalled my bag hanging on a chair in the diner.

Holding my breath, I listened. Both the corridor and shop remained quiet. What if Ryan had recovered from my assault and was creeping his way towards me? I quelled a scream and hurried towards the toilet.

I almost cried in relief when the small cubicle flooded with light. Holding on to the sink, I stared at the ghost-like face in the mirror. It was a Friday afternoon in Leeds city centre; why was I being so melodramatic?'

Ryan wasn't a big man. He probably couldn't overpower me if I fought like a demon. And why would he even attack me in the first place? Nevertheless, the sense of danger persisted. Tia-Marie said Ryan had been cruel as a boy, and I'd seen him go for Graham with a broken bottle.

I toyed with fleeing through the fire exit, but I couldn't leave my bag in the diner. Besides, I was just being fanciful.

Wedging the toilet door open with the bin, the light illuminated most of the corridor, and I steeled myself to return.

Stepping back into the bright lights of the diner, with the jukebox back in action, my fears evaporated. Ryan was nowhere to be seen. He might even have left. I listened for a moment to the soothing harmonies of The Everly Brothers until a loud crash from the kitchen drowned them out.

I grabbed my bag. Why didn't I just leave? But Donny might have fallen over, had an accident perhaps? I ran towards the kitchen, but my steps faltered as a scream rang out from there.

Ryan's raised voice followed. 'I don't bleedin' care if he's injured, the fat lump of lard. He needs to pay if he wants me to keep my mouth shut. Otherwise, he's looking at prison for the rest of his life.'

Through the partially open door, I glimpsed Donny slumped on the floor. His ruddy complexion had turned white, and his arm hung at a curious angle. His eyes were closed, spittle dribbled from his mouth, and he softly whimpered.

Tracy was bending over him. 'Dad, are you okay? Can you hear me?' She turned to Ryan with anxious eyes. 'I think he's broken his arm. I don't even know if he's fully conscious. Should we call an ambulance?'

'Should we hell. I want money for keeping my mouth shut. Get some brandy down his neck. He's got his stash.' Ryan opened a cupboard and passed a bottle to Tracy.

After a couple of mouthfuls, Donny opened his eyes, and a dash of pink spread across his cheeks. 'Tracy, love. My arm hurts. What happened? The pain ... I can't stand it.'

'Dad, you fell over and landed on your arm.' She glared so fiercely at Ryan, I'd have bet my life he'd pushed Donny. 'Don't worry, we'll get you to the hospital.'

Ryan kicked Donny's foot. 'You don't get it, Trace, do you? The tight arse needs to pay if he doesn't want me running to the cops.'

Donny's eyes widened at the kick before his face crumpled.

Tracy leapt up. 'You leave my dad alone.'

'I'm not leaving till I get what's owed.' He booted Donny hard in the thigh.

Donny's voice shook. 'I don't know what you're talking about, Ryan, but don't you dare threaten me. I always said you weren't good enough for my daughter.'

Ryan laughed. 'What you gonna do, old man? Run me down in your fancy car, then drive away?'

'Don't worry, Dad. He doesn't know anything.'

'Wouldn't be too sure about that, babe.' Ryan blew his girlfriend a kiss. 'Your tongue runs away with you when you're drunk.'

She slapped his face. 'You bastard.'

Ryan snarled and shoved Tracy aside as if she were a doll. I revised my opinion of his strength. With fists clenched, he stood over Donny, who squealed like a pig in a slaughterhouse. It had gone much too far. I fumbled for my phone to call the police.

Vaguely aware of the operator asking which service I needed, I'd no time to answer. Tracy launched herself at Ryan, but he threw her off and circled his hands around her throat. I had to take action.

Charging into the kitchen, I seized the first heavy object and smashed a medium-sized cast-iron pan over Ryan's head. He went down like a cartoon character. Stunned by my success, I imagined an egg-sized lump on his head in the morning. His body had fallen on the very spot where Graham had lain dead that Saturday morning. Breathing like a steam train and expecting Tracy's heartfelt thanks, I turned to face her.

She almost spat in my face. 'What have you done now, you interfering bitch?' She'd asked a similar question, if not quite as aggressively, when she'd found me washing the knife that killed Graham.

'I've just saved you from your violent boyfriend. Why was he demanding money?'

'None of your business.'

Donny piped up from the corner. 'I don't know what all that was about with Ryan, but you've saved our bacon, Helen.'

'Try not to talk, Dad, and I'll get you to the hospital.'

Forgetting I'd possibly already got the emergency services on the line, I asked if she intended to call an ambulance. Ryan lay spark out on the floor. Maybe he needed one, too?

Tracy didn't answer. She stared at me as if trying to read my mind. My jumbled, outlandish thoughts were probably written all over my face.

Ryan demanding money to save Donny from a lifetime in prison could only mean one thing. Had Donny deliberately run Liz down two years ago and then murdered Graham?

But vain, silly Donny couldn't be a murderer. Or could he? The police held Pauline in custody. Her prints had been on the knife. But my prints had been on it too.

Ryan lying there so still took me back to that morning again, with Tracy pointing at the knife and saying, "You should have left it ... there ... in the body".

I willed myself to return to the present.

Tracy had turned her back and was rummaging in a drawer. 'Dad, I'm going to give you some painkillers.'

He moaned. Ryan remained still. God, what if I'd killed him? It was less than a minute since I'd knocked him out, but it seemed like an age. I should have pushed for an ambulance, but it was my only chance to find out the truth.

'Tracy, I need to ask you something.'

She spun around. 'What?'

'That morning when you found me with the knife at the sink, why did you say I should have left it in the body? I didn't take it out.'

'Pauline did, then. So what?'

'But how did you know the knife had been left in the body? Did you arrive before me and see it?' *No, that couldn't be it. Try again.* 'Had you been there when ...?' I thought back to Ryan extorting money from Donny. 'Tracy, if you're trying to protect someone, it won't work.'

She darted her eyes at Donny and then back to me. 'Just shut up, will you? You interfering cow.'

As panic entered her eyes, my jumbled thoughts clicked into place, and I couldn't stop my words tumbling out. 'The thing is, only the murderer could have known they'd left the knife in the body.'

Tracy gave a deep sigh. 'I knew you'd eventually work it out. That's why ...' Baring her teeth, she raised her arm and pointed Donny's sharpest knife at my chest.

Mummy Dearest

With my knees shaking, I stepped back, but as if we'd choreographed a dreadful dance together, Tracy moved forward. She held the knife like a dagger. Groping for a shield, I pushed the hot dog steamer between us.

I'd already slipped my phone into my pocket. The emergency services had probably curtailed my call, but I needed to hope someone was there.

I dug my nails into my palms, and although fireworks were exploding in my head, I willed myself to keep calm. My voice came out in a hoarse whisper. 'Tracy, why are you holding that knife?'

The knife wobbled in her shaking hand. 'You've given me no choice. I'm going to have to kill you.'

I fought against my rising panic. *Keep her talking.* 'Like you killed Graham?'

'Yes, Miss Smarty Pants.' She puffed herself up as if expecting me to praise her.

Donny gasped. 'No, my baby. Not you. Pauline did it.'

Still aiming the knife at me, Tracy threw an anguished look at Donny. 'I didn't mean to stab him. It all got out of hand. Graham started ranting about you and Liz. He was going to rake up all that about ... you know ... said he was going to go to the police. I told him Liz's death was an accident.'

An accident? Did that mean Donny had run Liz over? My fuddled mind would hardly work. What was it Ryan had said?

Donny groaned. 'Graham threatened you and—'

Tears streamed down Tracy's face. 'He mocked me. Said I must be brain-dead to believe anything you said. Said you were evil, and I was a pathetic daddy's girl. Called me stupid. He cornered me in the kitchen, jabbing me with his fingers as he sneered. I don't ... I can't remember picking up the knife.'

I almost pitied the girl. Maybe I could persuade her I was on her side? 'Tracy, you could claim it was self-defence. As Donny said, Graham threatened you and—'

Tracy lunged at me, and I froze. 'Shut it, you interfering bitch. You've said enough.'

My empathy vanished. That hadn't got me anywhere. I flashed my eyes at Donny. Why didn't he try to talk her down?' He turned his head away. Riled, I couldn't stop myself from saying, 'Tracy is letting Pauline take the rap. What do you think about that, Donny?'

He didn't reply.

Tracy moved even closer so that the knife dug into my side. 'Keep your nose out of our family business. Dad loves me more than her. And Pauline taking the blame, so what? She was making a fool of herself over Graham while married to Dad. She deserves everything she gets.'

Tracy's warped view made my chest go tight. 'I've got a theory about Pauline,' I said, hoping Tracy would take the bait. It was little more than a wild guess from what Donny had said – or, at least, what he'd nearly said. To pique her interest, I added, 'Your dad might confirm it.'

Tracy breathed hard, and the tendons bulged in her neck. 'Look, you thick cow, I don't give a toss about her.'

'Pauline knows the truth but wants to protect you because ...' I fixed my gaze on Donny. 'Do you want to tell her?'

Even though he shook his head, the flicker in his eyes said I'd guessed right.

'Tell me what?'

I softened my voice. 'Pauline's your real mother. Valerie couldn't have children. Your dad told me.' *At least he almost did.*

Tracy furrowed her brow. 'Don't be so bloody stupid. You don't know what you're talking about. Dad, tell her she's ...'

Closing his eyes, Donny clutched his arm and moaned. His face had lost its colour again, and his moustache hung like a rat's tail.

'I know your pathetic game, Helen,' snarled Tracy. 'You must think I'm stupid; just like Graham did.'

Even though chilled by her words, I persisted. 'So how are you going to explain my death? You can't pin that on Pauline – your mother.'

Tracy stamped her foot. 'That miserable cow is not my bloody mother.' She gestured to Ryan. 'This scumbag threatened my dad. He's gonna pay for that. I'll say he went berserk. Killed you and attacked us. And little old me knocked him out. The knife will be next to him, covered in his prints. See! I'm not so stupid after all.'

I needed to move, to make a run for it, but my feet were planted like dumbbells. *Come on, Helen. Move.*

The kitchen door had closed behind me. If I turned, Tracy would stab me in the back. She had me cornered like an animal.

I'd not only frozen in fright, but heavy inertia pressed down on my shoulders. Who would care if I died? Would Zack come back for my funeral, or would he not think it worth the flight?

As tears flooded my eyes, I'd almost resigned myself to the inevitable, but Tracy's complacent smile inflamed me.

I found myself shouting. 'Tracy, look! Donny's having a seizure.'

As she whipped around to face him, I pushed her solid form with all my might. She tottered in her high heels, and it bought me the time to fling open the door and enter the shop. I ran the length of the counter.

The lights shone brightly. Passers-by on the busy street could see in. I'd hoped that would deter Tracy, but the sound of a raging bull at my heels said otherwise.

At the end of the counter, I stumbled, then screamed as she grabbed my shirt. More agile than Tracy, I pulled free and headed towards the windows. Grabbing one of the interview chairs, I swung it around in a circle before launching it at her.

Tracy batted it off. 'You can't get away from me,' she mocked. 'Bet you wish you had your skates on.' Her demented laugh rang out. 'Not that they'd have saved you. Bloody useless, you were on them.'

I didn't waste my breath replying. Not when it seemed in such short supply. As I reached for another chair to fling, I glimpsed a shape at the window. This second chair hit Tracy's ample middle and sufficiently winded her so that I could run back to the coffee machine.

After supporting myself against it for a second or so, I grabbed what I'd come for, and as a bellowing Tracy charged, I flung one of my new, metal roller skates at her head. She jerked to one side, and the skate flew past. I had one chance left. *Don't waste it, Helen.*

Instead of flinging the other skate, I wound the long laces around my shaking hand and swung the heavy skate into her face. Tracy staggered, but she was still aiming the knife at me. This time, I pulled my arm back and smacked her with greater force. Sinking to her knees and howling, she dropped the knife. I kicked it to the other side of the room.

I couldn't resist a few taunting words. 'How did I do with the skates, Trace? Turns out I'm pretty hot after all.'

With knees still knocking, I lurched towards the exit. The door opened, and a pair of outstretched arms caught me as I collapsed.

In a Budget Hotel

I'd fallen into the arms of Constable Harper. Handing me to a milk-faced Jade, he strode towards Tracy, clapped on the handcuffs, and attached her to the foot rail of the counter.

After reciting the caution in a robotic voice, he returned, wearing a huge smile. 'That's the first person I've disarmed and arrested for attempted murder. Wait till the lads hear about this.'

Jade ran to hug him.

My legs gave way, and I sank into a chair. 'Hello,' I called. 'I'm still here. The victim, you know.'

It became a blur after that. A multitude of emergency vehicles and personnel descended. Both Ryan and Donny were carried out on stretchers, and the paramedics patched up Tracy before the police whisked her away. I had to return to the station to make a statement. Constable Harper's boss, Dracula, kept me for ages, going through the same points over and over again.

I lounged in bed for most of the next day. During a brief conversation with James, I tried to make light of my ordeal. And I certainly didn't tell him how fatalistic I'd felt in the face of death. There was everything to live for today.

'One last night at the hotel,' I said. 'Then back to Buttersley and Prue. I'll be sad to leave my new friends. We're having a catch-up at the hotel tonight.'

'Sounds a blast.' He seemed distracted. 'Sorry. Got to go. Busy at work and all that. Speak to you soon.'

He rang off before I could answer. My buoyancy dipped.

After packing my few clothes, I went down to the bar and waited for Gloria and Jade with a bottle of Prosecco on ice. I almost shed a tear when they stood in the doorway peering in.

After nudging each other and pointing, they rushed to my table. Jade plonked herself down, bursting with importance. She couldn't wait to detail the praise Constable Harper had received from his bosses.

'First on the scene, he was. His quick thinking ...' Jade held up her palm. 'No, Glo, don't say anything. He saved Helen's life. Matter of fact, we both did. It was me who dragged him there in the first place.'

I'd already disabled Tracy and escaped the danger, but I didn't have the heart to burst Jade's bubble.

'I've never been so glad to see anyone,' I said.

Jade directed her triumphant smile at Gloria. 'There you are, you see. *You* weren't there.'

'No, I'll give you that. But I've spoken to someone significantly involved in the affair.'

Jade pouted. 'Who?'

'Pauline.' Gloria sat back.

'You haven't.' I said. 'How? When?'

'Wasn't sure she'd been released, but I phoned her on the off-chance this morning to ask how she was. Turns out she needed a shoulder to cry on, and I was the one to get drenched.'

My mouth hung open. What to ask first? I could hardly get my words out quickly enough. 'What did she tell you about the night of the party?'

Gloria drained her glass. 'So, the Donoghues had their meeting after everyone left and agreed to put all the bad feeling behind them.'

'Was Ryan at the meeting?' I asked. 'I take it Graham was there?'

'She said Ryan left. Graham *was* there but seemed preoccupied. He hardly spoke. When the meeting broke up, Pauline overheard him saying he wanted a word with Tracy. Donny and Pauline left, and Tracy said she would lock up.'

I signalled for another bottle. 'When first interviewed by the police, Tracy must have been obliged to admit she stayed behind with Graham?'

'You'd think so, wouldn't you?' said Gloria. 'But initially, you were in the frame, and then Pauline, so they weren't looking at her.'

Jade rapped the table with her knuckles. 'That's because Pauline told the police she'd done it.' Swivelling her head between us, she added, 'You didn't know that, did you? Shall I tell you why she confessed?'

Not wanting to spoil her delight, I feigned ignorance. Gloria possibly knew, but she just smiled and raised her brow.

Jade paused for effect. 'Pauline is Tracy's real mother. But Tracy didn't know. Can you believe it?'

We both looked at the floor.

'You knew, didn't you?' Jade blew out her cheeks and slumped in the seat.

Gloria patted her hand. 'Nice to have it officially confirmed. Yes, Pauline told me. Before meeting Graham, she got pregnant from a one-night stand with Donny. After the birth, she suffered from postnatal depression. Alone and skint, she couldn't cope. By then, Donny had married Valerie, and they offered to give the child a stable, family home. Valerie insisted that no one should know she wasn't the mother. At the time, Pauline thought it was for the best, but she's regretted it ever since.'

'Poor Pauline,' I said. 'That's her tragedy. But to return to the night of the party, why did she go back to the diner?'

'Yeah,' Jade leaned forward. 'I want to know that too.'

'Okay,' said Gloria. 'On the drive home, Donny ranted about Graham and said Tracy was going to sort him out.'

Jade grabbed Gloria's arm. 'Do you think Donny encouraged her?'

She shrugged. 'I've always said he got others to do his dirty work.'

'Although Donny was injured when Tracy threatened me with the knife,' I said, 'he did nothing to stop her.' I put a steadying hand on my shaking knees. 'And Ryan seemed to think Donny was responsible. He virtually accused him of killing Liz in that hit-and-run.'

Jade nodded like a wise judge. 'That's why the police are looking into her death again. Ryan clammed up when interviewed. Said he'd lost his memory from the bang on the head. But my Matt reckons Ryan knows something, and he'll get it out of him if anyone can.'

I exchanged a quick smile with Gloria while we dwelled on the expertise of Constable Harper.

'Sorry,' said Jade. 'You were telling us about Pauline.'

'Oh, yes. Where was I? She and Donny continued arguing when they got home. When he went to bed, Pauline felt unnerved by it all and wanted to speak to Graham. He didn't answer his mobile or landline, and she rang loads. This made her even more agitated, so she jumped back in the car and drove to Graham's house. It was in darkness. She banged so hard on the door, she woke the neighbours, but Graham wasn't there. Then she drove to the diner.'

'I can take it from there,' said Jade. 'Pauline now admits she found Graham's body with the knife still in the wound. She pulled it out, thinking she might save him, but it was far too late. Then she panicked and ran out. Later, when she'd calmed down, she realised Tracy must have killed him.'

'Happy for me to take the blame though, wasn't she?' I slammed my glass onto the table. 'That must have been an unexpected bonus, and I've been feeling sorry for her.'

Gloria put her arm around my shoulders. 'Don't take it so personally. She would have been desperate for her daughter. The thing is, I know Tracy's not the brightest spark, but how did she think she could get away with it? She wasn't to know Pauline would take the blame.'

Jade shrieked and clutched my arm. 'But she knew Helen would arrive first in the morning. Maybe she hoped to pin it on you all along, Hels?' Pleased with her theory, she released my arm. 'Tracy never liked you.'

I sighed. 'And I played into her hands by picking up the knife. She couldn't call the police quickly enough.'

'But why kill Graham in the first place?' asked Gloria.

'I don't think she meant to kill him,' I said. 'In her words, it got out of hand. And I'm not sure what to make of Liz's death. Tracy called it an accident. That's what she believed, anyway.'

Gloria wrinkled her brow. 'So it wasn't to shut him up, then?'

Gazing at the ceiling, I drummed my fingers. 'Maybe? But it was perhaps more complicated than that. You've just said she's not the brightest spark. And I think she's insecure. Got a chip on her shoulder. Graham goaded her. It had been an eventful night. She just lost it and stabbed him in temper, fear and ... oh, I don't know.'

Gloria snorted. 'Had the presence of mind to wipe the knife clean, though, didn't she? As for that rat, Donny—'

Time to change the subject. 'By the way, do you know if my call to the emergency services remained open?'

Jade nodded. 'Yes, they've got it all on record. The police were on their way, but my Matt got there first.'

'Lucky for me,' I said. 'Has Tracy—'

'Don't look now, but a gorgeous man at the bar is staring at us.' Gloria flashed her eyes and jiggled her brows. 'A bit young for me, but I'd give him a whirl.'

Ignoring Gloria's instruction, Jade whipped her head around. 'Too old for me, but he's hot. Not as nice as my Matt, though.'

I refused to join the fan club. 'Will you two stop it? We've got serious things to discuss.'

Jade yawned. 'Thought we were done?'

'If you're bored, go get us another drink,' said Gloria. 'These bottles don't go far.'

As Jade skipped off to the bar, I told Gloria I was returning to Buttersley.

'What about you, Glo? What are your plans? Donny can't reopen now. Not without Tracy, and I can't see Pauline going back there.'

She sighed. 'Look for another job, I suppose. One that'll fit in with the boys. I'll miss you.'

'Me too.' I covered her hand. 'But Buttersley's not far. We can still meet up.'

As both my friends were losing their jobs, I couldn't yet share my good news. Even Prue hadn't been able to contain her excitement when she told me Bright Sparks Electrics on Buttersley's high street had switched off for good.

'There's a sign in the window,' she'd said. 'And I wasted no time in bothering with the agents, but contacted the landlord. I went to school with his mother. You've got an appointment to see him on Monday morning.'

Jade plonked a bottle of Veuve Clicquot on the table. 'Surprise! That man at the bar sent it. He's coming over.'

'Wow,' said Gloria. 'He looks even better close up.'

Puzzled, I looked up to see a tall man walking towards me with his arms outstretched. Surely not? It couldn't be, could it?

I blinked, closed my eyes, and reopened them immediately. 'James! I can't believe it. What are *you* doing here in—?'

'A budget hotel? I've no idea. But I've come to keep my eye on you. You're not fit to be left on your own.'

The Golden Roller Skates Awards

Thanks to all my regular critique friends on Scribophile for
their
constructive advice and all-round brilliance.
Leslie, Jim, Sylvia, Ros, Corry, Chris M,
Chris R, CJW, MJC, Effie, Sam.
And special thanks to my cozy writing buddy, Christa Bakker

Thanks also to eagle-eyed Lee from Bookediting.co.uk
and Tiffany @writenowcreative.com for the extra emotion.